Don't Speak!

Sherlock gave a bark, which Amy supposed meant "OK," or, "I understand," or maybe even "I don't like it," but why didn't he just say so? And why was he looking beyond her instead of at her?

Reluctantly, fearing the worst, Amy turned around.

And saw Sean Gorman standing there. With his eyes wide. And his mouth hanging open. Which pretty much killed any hope Amy might have had that he hadn't heard Sherlock speaking.

"How . . ." Sean said. "What . . . I . . ."

Maybe insanity runs in his family, Amy thought, and she could make him believe he'd been hearing voices.

"Yes?" she said innocently.

Sean turned back to Sherlock. "How do you do that?" he demanded. "How do you know how to talk?"

Amy fought the urge to say, "He's that new breed of Mexican Speaking Spaniel." Sean wasn't going to believe anything except the truth. "He's a science experiment. And the scientists are out to get him—to cut open his brain to see how it works. If you tell anybody, you could get him killed."

Sherlock approached slowly and let Sean pet him.

"I won't tell anybody," Sean assured them both.

SMART DOG

SMART DOG

by Vivian Vande Velde

SCHOLASTIC INC.

New York Toronto London Auckland Sydney
Mexico City New Delhi Hong Kong Buenos Aires

ISBN-13: 978-0-545-06070-7
ISBN-10: 0-545-06070-2

12 11 10 9 8 7 6 5 4   8 9 10 11 12 13/0

Printed in the U.S.A.   40

First Scholastic printing, February 2008

Text set in Fairfield Medium
Designed by Lydia D'moch

To Elizabeth,
who always wanted a smart dog

Contents

SMART
DOG

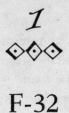

1

F-32

Amy Prochenko had her walk to school timed perfectly.

If she was too slow, she'd arrive late and get detention—not to mention a lecture from her teacher, her principal, and her parents, in that order. If she was too quick, she'd get there before her friends. Complicating things was the fact that the two or three girls she usually hung around with all lived far enough away that they rode buses, which could be unpredictable.

Arriving ahead of her friends wouldn't have been so bad except that the very first person to get to school every morning was Kaitlyn Walker, whose mother dropped her off early on her way to work. Kaitlyn was the most popular girl in the fifth grade—

looked up to, fussed over, and imitated by all the in crowd. Amy was so far removed from the in crowd that Kaitlyn wouldn't talk to her even if they were the only two people in the room.

Amy knew that for a fact because it had happened.

One by one, fifth-grade girls and boys alike would enter, and gather around Kaitlyn, and start making fun of Amy.

That had happened, too.

So Amy preferred to get to school between five and seven minutes before the eight o'clock bell. This gave her time to settle in, with enough other people there—people who were not from the in crowd—for Kaitlyn to have a full range of targets.

On this particular spring morning as Amy walked to school, she was well within her schedule when she saw a dog sitting on the sidewalk. It was a medium-sized dog with floppy ears and big brown eyes and long fur that was equal parts brown and white and black.

"Excuse me," the dog said just as Amy was about to step around him. "I'm in trouble. Could you please help me?"

Amy stopped, panicked—not because she was afraid, for the dog wasn't scary—but because she had no idea how to react. She knew dogs didn't talk, but probably the last thing she would have expected a dog to say if it *could* talk was "Excuse me" and "Please." She wouldn't have guessed that a dog would be so polite. Her family had never had dogs, so maybe it wasn't fair for her to judge; but from what she had seen, dogs tended to eat out of garbage cans, bark all night, and poop where people were most likely to step. None of these struck her as indications of deep thinking. Yet here was this dog, speaking in a grumbly-barky but easy-to-understand voice, asking politely and intelligently for help.

She glanced around, although she already knew there was nobody else nearby and that, in any case, the voice had definitely come from the dog. Still she looked, for she knew that dogs don't normally speak— politely or not—and she hated to appear foolish, even if the dog was the only witness.

She saw she had been right: She and the dog were the only ones in sight.

So she stepped closer and asked, "What kind of trouble? Are you lost?"

The dog shook his head, making the metal tags on his collar jingle. "Just the opposite," he said. "I'm trying to get lost."

Amy checked the tags anyway because she didn't know where else to start. One was shiny red and had a date engraved: August 17 of last year. The other was unpainted, and it was engraved with the number F-32. "What are these?" she asked.

"The red one shows that my rabies shots are up to date," the dog said.

This was good news to Amy, who suddenly remembered that the police officer who had talked to her class about safety had warned never to approach an animal that was acting strangely. She would have to admit that a dog stopping her and asking for help was strange.

The dog continued, "And the other one is my name tag."

Amy flipped over the tag that said F-32. On the other side was a telephone number and the words:

State College of New York at Rochester
Research Department
Rochester, New York 14619

She didn't think either side made a good name. "Your name is F-32?" she asked.

"Yes," the dog answered.

Definitely not a good name.

Amy said, "And you belong to someone at the college?"

Again F-32 shook his head, pulling the tag out from Amy's hand. He scratched himself—but discreetly, for a dog. "I belong to the college itself," he corrected.

To the Research Department, Amy thought. And then suddenly everything was clear to her. "You're a science experiment," she guessed, which was the only explanation for why the dog was smart enough to talk. "And you're—"

F-32 nodded. "Running away," he finished. "Yes. Will you help me?"

$\mathcal{2}$
◈◆◈

THE LAB

"I ran away from home once when I was seven," Amy told F-32. "I was only gone for an hour, because when I was seven I wasn't allowed to cross the street, so I hid in Julie Duran's garage. But my parents got real worried and called the police and my mother was crying and everything. I felt terrible."

The dog listened to her with his head cocked to one side and didn't interrupt.

Amy said, "The people at the college are probably worried about you." But then she remembered that the reason she had run away was because she'd been angry that her parents wouldn't let her go to the PG-13 movie she had wanted to see, and that wasn't a very likely reason for a dog to run away. She tried to think like a dog and asked, "Or were they mean to you?"

F-32 paused to consider. "No," he said slowly. "During the day we'd do all sorts of fun and interesting things, and the students always scratched my belly every time I rolled over." He wagged his tail, sweeping the sidewalk, at the thought. "I really like having my belly scratched," he added wistfully. "But at night they would go home, and they'd lock me in my cage in the lab and I'd be all alone, except for the night guard. And they told me not to talk to him because I was a secret experiment."

"Oh," Amy said, sad at the thought of being locked up.

"I didn't tell them that I'd figured out the cage latch back when I was still a puppy. That was *my* secret experiment. It wasn't the cage that bothered me so much. It was that when they weren't working, sometimes the people would go to parties together, or do things together and talk and laugh about it the next day, but I *always* had to stay in the lab."

"That's the worst thing, to feel left out," Amy agreed. She thought of Kaitlyn Walker.

"It *was*," F-32 said. "Then last week I overheard Dr. Boden, who's in charge of the lab, talking into his tape recorder, where he dictates his notes. He was whispering when he thought I couldn't hear. That's what made me interested, so I listened." The dog lowered *his* voice, and Amy crouched down to hear better. "He said I'd gotten as smart as I was going to get, and now he wanted to see how my brain worked. I couldn't tell why he was making it into a secret, but then he said that before the end of the semester they were going to dissect my brain. Just then he looked up and saw me, and immediately he turned the recorder off and started doing something else. I didn't know what *dissect* meant, but he looked so worried I might have overheard, I remembered the word and looked it up on the lab computer that night. It means they're going to cut open my brain to examine it."

"That's terrible!" Amy cried. Then she asked, amazed, "You know how to use a computer?"

F-32 nodded. "I don't think I'm supposed to, because they never actually showed me how. But I watched the students play computer games when the professors weren't there; and I taught myself, at night, between the guard's rounds. I like games. And I like knocking over that little garbage can that's in the corner of the screen, to go through and see what people have thrown out. I have to hold a pencil between my teeth and press the keys with the eraser end because my paws are too big."

"You *are* smart," Amy said.

"Thank you." F-32 wagged his tail proudly. "But when I learned what the people were planning, I decided I better not act so smart. So when they explained their tests, I pretended I couldn't understand and made mistakes. And I started chasing my tail and bumping into things—like the outside dogs."

"Outside dogs?" Amy repeated.

"Dogs that don't belong to the college," F-32 explained. "There's a window in the lab, and sometimes

I could see dogs and their people playing on the hill, fetching sticks or balls or Frisbees. It looked like fun, but Dr. Boden said *that* was a waste of time and it was just for stupid dogs." He cocked his head and looked at Amy quizzically.

"It's still fun," Amy said. "But anyway, acting not-so-smart sounds like a good plan, so they'd want to study you longer."

"Except that everybody got worried that something was going wrong, and Dr. Boden decided to check my brain out right away. I think he might have suspected that I had caught on, because that time he spelled it out on the recorder. Spelling is my worst subject. But I could make out 'd-i-s-s-e-c-t' and 't-o-m-o-r-r-o-w.' "

"That's awful," Amy said. She felt sorry for the dog, angry at the college researchers, and determined to do something. "Of course I'll help you get away from those terrible people."

"Thank you," F-32 said. "What should we do first?"

That was a disappointment because Amy had assumed he'd have a plan, since he was so smart. But he just waited for her, scratching under his collar, which made his tags jingle.

Amy wasn't used to people depending on her, expecting her to come up with plans. She preferred clearly explained rules and to be told what to do, like coloring within the lines in a coloring book rather than designing a drawing of her own. Now, for inspiration, she thought of TV shows she'd seen. On TV, police officers were always going undercover, so that was where she would start. "First," Amy said, "we'll get rid of your identification." She unbuckled his collar and stuffed it into her backpack. "What does F-32 mean, anyway?" She took a sudden breath. "Are there other animals in danger?" she asked. "Are there animals named A through F, and one to thirty-two?"

"No," F-32 said. "*F* is for Frank, which is Dr. Boden's other name. Thirty-two is the room number for the lab in the Science Building."

"Then it's an even worse name than I thought," Amy said, outraged that the dog should be named for his owner and location. "So, second is we have to give you a different name."

"You mean a word name," F-32 asked in a tone of wonder and delight, "instead of a number name?"

Amy had to smile at how such a little thing could please him so much.

But then he continued, "Like Dr. Boden and Karen and Tiffany and Denzel and—"

Amy interrupted. "You don't want to name yourself after people who would dissect someone just for being smart. You're the smartest dog that ever was, so you should be named after the smartest person there ever was."

"Who's that?" F-32 asked.

Amy thought for a moment, weighing King Solomon against Leonardo da Vinci, both of whom she'd learned about in school that year. But neither seemed exactly right. "Sherlock Holmes," she said. "He's a famous detective who could figure out anything."

"Like the computer, and the locks," F-32 said.

Amy nodded. "Exactly. Would you like me to call you Sherlock?"

"Sherlock sounds like a fine name," F-32 said. "What's your name?"

"Amy Prochenko."

"Pleased to meet you, Amy," Sherlock said. He held up his paw, and they shook.

BEHAVING

W hat do we do next?" Sherlock asked.

Amy was suddenly jerked back from the world of undercover cops and London detectives. *Next?*

Uh-oh.

She didn't have a watch, but she could guess the time.

"Oh no," she said. "I'm on my way to school, and I'm already going to be late from talking so long."

Sherlock shuddered at the mention of school. "Do the people at your school experiment on animals?" he asked in a tone that said he was wondering if he'd made the right choice after all in asking her for help.

"Of course not!" Amy said. "We don't even *have* animals. Well, except Mrs. Battersby's room has an aquarium, but that's just so the second graders can learn about feeding fish and keeping the water clean and that sort of thing."

"No experiments?" Sherlock repeated.

"No experiments," Amy assured him.

Sherlock wagged his tail and began to circle around Amy. "Then I'd love to go to school," he told her. "School is fun. Do you go through mazes and have to remember which door the food is behind? I'm good at that. I'm not very good at spelling."

"Our school has more spelling than that other stuff," Amy said. She started to walk. Fast. "Besides, animals aren't allowed."

"The fish are," Sherlock objected. "Everybody's heard of schools of fish."

"That's not the same thing at all," Amy told him. "Anyway, the fish just sit in their bowl and swim around quietly all day."

"How do they learn, if they aren't allowed to ask questions?"

"They aren't there to learn," Amy said. "Only the children are."

"I should think the fish would get bored," Sherlock said, "and complain."

Amy shook her head. "Fish aren't smart enough to complain. You have no idea how much smarter you are than ordinary animals. They can't talk."

"I know that," Sherlock said, but Amy wasn't convinced. Especially when he added, muttering, "I bet the fish complain to each other."

She said, "And most animals can't understand

very much, either. Except some dogs and cats know things like 'Sit,' and 'Food,' and maybe their own name. Or maybe not."

Sherlock wrinkled his nose at the mention of cats. But all he said was, "I can sit quiet as a fish."

"You still wouldn't be allowed," Amy told him. "You'll have to wait outside the building until school's out for the day." She had another thought. "And you'll have to make sure people don't see you. Since you don't have a collar, someone might call Animal Control to pick you up and lock you away, and that's the first place those research people would look for you."

"Why?" Sherlock asked.

"*Why*, what?" Sherlock's questions kept distracting her from worrying about being late.

"Why would they call Animal Control because I don't have a collar?"

"Because then you might be a stray dog, and they'd be afraid you'd bite people."

"Not biting was one of the first lessons I learned," Sherlock told her in the same tone Amy would have used to assure someone she had long ago stopped needing a diaper.

"But people worry," Amy said. "Especially around kids. People want to make sure dogs are friendly."

Sherlock positively grinned and wagged his tail.

"Very friendly," Amy admitted. "Stay hidden anyway. Here's the school." She stopped in front of the long, brick building. The doors were closed and everybody was already inside. "You can stay in these bushes." The yard that bordered the school was very overgrown, and Amy estimated two or three dogs could hide and not be noticed for a week.

If they behaved themselves.

"Behave," she warned. "I'll be back at 2:30 when school lets out."

"I'll behave," Sherlock said. He lay down quietly and rested his head on his paws, looking the picture of good behavior.

The school bell rang just as Amy ran up to the front door, making her officially late.

LATE

Sister Mary Grace was writing the names of Native American tribes on the blackboard when Amy rushed into the classroom. Sister Mary Grace made a point of looking at the wall clock. She shook her head, but said mildly, "Amy, we just this minute gave up on you. If you hurry, you can catch Kaitlyn on her way to the office and cross your name off the absence list, so you don't get marked late."

Luckily, it was a small school, with only one floor. Amy could see Kaitlyn at the end of the hall, about to turn the corner. Running wasn't allowed, but Amy was certain she'd be able to catch up because Kaitlyn was walking along slowly, making sure that she was noticed as she passed those classrooms that had their doors open. Kaitlyn was so popular even the sixth graders knew her.

The younger kids probably knew her, too, but they didn't count.

Moving along at a pace just short of running, Amy followed Kaitlyn around the corner. Kaitlyn had paused to admire her reflection in the glass of the trophy case. There was a lot to admire. Kaitlyn had perfect hair, perfect teeth, a big enough wardrobe that she rarely wore the same outfit twice, and a figure just as good as the girls who played soccer—except that she didn't play sports, which gave her the added advantage of no sweat.

"Kaitlyn," Amy called, not daring to shout, but raising her voice so that Mr. Dambra, whose room she was passing, scowled and closed his door.

Amy thought Kaitlyn must have heard, for she seemed to glance over her shoulder, but maybe she was just tossing her perfect hair, for she started walking again—much faster than before.

"Kaitlyn," Amy called a second time.

Was she deaf, or what? Kaitlyn disappeared into the office, two doors ahead of where Amy was.

When Amy walked into the office, she saw that all was not lost. Kaitlyn was waiting for Mrs. Jensen, the secretary, who was busy talking on the phone.

"Kaitlyn," Amy said a third time—

—just as Kaitlyn tossed the absence list on Mrs. Jensen's desk.

Then, finally, Kaitlyn turned around. "Oh," she said,

her voice dripping with sweetness and innocence. "Amy." She smiled brightly. "Love your sweater."

The way she said it made Amy look down to make sure it didn't have a stain or catch and that it hadn't ridden up while she'd been chasing after Kaitlyn. Amy had worn the same sweater at least once a week since the weather had turned cool in October, and now here it was the week before Easter. If Kaitlyn had truly liked it, she'd had plenty of chances to say so before.

Now Kaitlyn said, "I've heard if you wait long enough, all the old styles come back." Her smile faltered, as though she was thinking that from now on she wouldn't believe all that she heard. "Oh well!" she added brightly, and breezed past Amy.

Watching Kaitlyn promenade down the hall, Amy thought Kaitlyn was the kind of person who proved your mother was wrong when you were worried about your hair or clothes or something foolish you'd done, and your mother said, "Oh, don't worry. Nobody noticed; nobody cares."

Amy forced herself to stop watching Kaitlyn.

Mrs. Jensen was still talking on the telephone, looking flustered; apparently whoever was on the other end was giving her a hard time.

Would it be rude to reach over and take the absence list? Amy was just trying to talk her fingers into moving, when Mrs. Jensen picked up the page and began fanning herself with it.

Amy was feeling hot and sticky herself.

After four or five minutes, Mrs. Jensen finally straightened out the problem, whatever it was, and hung up the phone.

"Now," she said, "Amy. What can I do for you?"

Finally. "I'm present," Amy said. "Sister Mary Grace has me on the absence report."

Mrs. Jensen glanced at the wall clock and crossed Amy's name off the absence list. And wrote it down on a sheet labeled TARDY. "Try to be on time," she recommended, as though Amy had never thought of that.

5

MISBEHAVING

*D*uring silent reading, Amy became aware that there was very little silence or reading going on. There was, instead, a great deal of giggling and poking. Amy figured that Kaitlyn was probably doing what Kaitlyn did best: gleefully tormenting someone, much to the entertainment of the other fifth graders. *As long as it's someone else,* Amy thought. She felt guilty for the thought, but not guilty enough to get involved.

But then she noticed that—in addition to the giggling and poking—there was also a lot of pointing in the direction of the windows.

Amy, whose desk was three rows away from the windows, glanced up and saw nothing.

Then she saw Sherlock's grinning face appear in one of the windows.

Then she saw nothing.

Then she saw Sherlock's grinning face reappear.

Then she saw nothing.

Amy closed her eyes then opened them again—as though she could possibly have been mistaken in what she'd seen, as though anything else could be mistaken for a medium-sized brown, white, and black dog leaping up and down as though he were on a trampoline. For a smart dog, Amy thought as Sherlock jumped back into view, he was looking pretty silly.

He must have remembered her saying that people were nervous about stray dogs biting, because he was working very hard at looking friendly: head cocked to one side, tongue hanging out, ears flopping, all the while grinning foolishly. Obviously he knew that the children could see him, and obviously he loved being the center of attention. Amy was sure that was an expression of delight on his face when he saw that she'd noticed him.

She shook her head, but he didn't catch the hint to go away. She covered her face with her book to let him know she didn't want to see him. From the continuing laughter of the other children, he didn't catch on to that, either.

"Class," Sister Mary Grace said in her warning voice.

No, no, no, no, Amy wished.

She sat very straight and quiet, with her book held up in front of her to show Sister Mary Grace that she was concentrating on her work.

But it didn't work. One out of thirty must not have been enough. Sister Mary Grace put down her own book and headed for the windows.

Amy silently mouthed the words "Go away."

Apparently, smart as Sherlock was, he wasn't smart enough to read lips. Or at least not while he was bouncing up and down on the school lawn.

At least, Amy thought, *Sister Mary Grace seems more puzzled than angry.* In fact—Amy started breathing again—Sister Mary Grace began to laugh. She liked to say that she had been a teacher for almost forty years, and there wasn't much she hadn't seen or heard before. Now she tapped on the glass and pretended to scold. "Dogs go to dog school; people go to people school. Those dogs who want to play with people will have to wait until recess after lunch, and that isn't for another forty-five minutes. Do you understand?"

Don't answer! Amy frantically wished at Sherlock.

Sherlock must have remembered that dogs couldn't talk. He barked, once, and stopped jumping.

"Very good," Sister Mary Grace said. "You *are* a clever dog, aren't you?"

Sherlock gave another sharp bark.

"Now, no more barking," Sister Mary Grace said. "You just wait quietly until recess." She laughed again, and Sean Gorman, whose desk was in the first row, reported to the rest of the class, "He's lying down, just like he can understand exactly what Sister said."

Good, Amy thought. *Let's hope he* obeys *Sister better than he obeys me.*

He must at least have given the impression that he would, for Sister Mary Grace said, "Now if I could only get my class to behave so well."

She should have known better.

Instantly several of the children started barking, or sat panting, tongues hanging out while they pretended to beg.

"Just my luck," Sister Mary Grace said, shaking her head. "The good dog's outside, and the misbehaving dogs are inside."

Which sounded—even to Amy—like an invitation to act like a dog.

It was the end of silent reading for that day.

6

❖❖❖

RECESS

At lunch Amy gulped down her sandwich and ignored the people she usually ate with so that she could be first in line at recess. But Sherlock came trotting over as soon as the yelling, laughing children burst out of the doors onto the playground, and someone shouted, "Look! There's that dog!" And then Amy wasn't first anymore.

Several children surged past Amy, but it was Kaitlyn whose voice carried. "Here, doggy, doggy, doggy," Kaitlyn said, in the kind of singsong voice people sometimes use with babies.

But Sherlock walked right by her to stand in front of Amy, which made Amy blush with pride.

Kaitlyn tossed her hair, to show she didn't really care.

"Wait, wait!" Sister Mary Grace called, suddenly concerned now that the children were actually outside, with the dog in their midst. "Does anybody know who this animal belongs to?"

She'll call Animal Control for sure, Amy thought. And from there, the college research people would pick him up. Wishing she was smart enough to think up better choices than do nothing or say "He's mine," she took a deep breath and answered, "He's mine."

"Great!" some of the kids said, taking that as permission that they could play with him. "What else does he do? Does he know tricks? Jump, boy, jump!"

Sister Mary Grace looked as though she were about to give a dogs/people appropriate-places lecture, so Amy said, "I know he doesn't belong at school. He must have followed me." She turned to Sherlock, who was sitting patiently, looking up at her. "Bad dog," she said. "Bad, bad dog."

Sherlock hung his head as though ashamed.

Amy didn't believe it for a second.

"Can he shake hands?" somebody asked. "Give me your paw, boy. Can he roll over and play dead?"

Ignoring the enthusiastic children, Sister Mary Grace suggested hopefully, "Maybe one of your parents could pick him up?"

"They both work," Amy said, which was true. She didn't add the little detail that so far they didn't even know they had a dog. She'd worry later how she'd convince them that they needed one. The important thing for now was to keep Sister Mary Grace from calling Animal Control.

And Sister Mary Grace still looked doubtful. "Is he good with children?"

Sherlock wagged his tail and gave a friendly bark.

"Oh, yes," Amy assured her. "He's a bad, bad dog, but he's very good with children. He absolutely never bites or chases."

Sherlock barked and offered a paw to Sister Mary Grace.

"He's a *very* safe dog," Amy said.

Sister Mary Grace looked as though she was weakening.

Amy said, "And he doesn't like the heat." Luckily it was quite warm for spring. "If I bring him to that shady area on the other side of the fence"—Amy glared at Sherlock and spoke directly to him—*"I'm sure he'll stay."*

Sherlock rolled on the grass, exposing his belly, and the children groaned and begged Sister Mary Grace to allow him to stay on the playground.

Finally Sister Mary Grace caved in. "He can stay while Amy is out here," she said. "But put him on the other side of the fence when the younger children come out."

The children cheered. Amy was ready to hug her, but that was too big a reaction for what she was pretending was going on, so she only waved as Sister Mary Grace went back into the school.

Everything was beginning to look perfect.

Then Kaitlyn moved closer.

Kaitlyn made a show of holding her hand in front of her mouth, but her voice carried as she said to

Minneh Tannen, one of her friends, "Ever notice how after a while people and their dogs start to look alike?"

Amy felt her cheeks grow red as her classmates laughed and repeated Kaitlyn's comment. Not that Sherlock was a bad-looking dog, but Amy knew it was meant as an insult.

Sherlock cocked his head and looked from Amy to Kaitlyn, then back to Amy.

Sean Gorman, one of the few who had not laughed, asked, "What's your dog's name?" That was all she needed, to have Sean start talking to her— Sean, who was so smart he'd skipped the second half of fourth grade to join the fifth in January. He was even less popular than Amy because he was always raising his hand and volunteering answers.

"Sherlock," Amy muttered.

"Like the detective?" Sean asked.

Leave it to him to know, but Amy nodded, pleased she didn't have to explain.

Kaitlyn said, " 'Clueless' would be a better name."

"He's a smart dog," somebody said.

"Not if he thinks he's a kangaroo," Kaitlyn jeered.

Sherlock barked at her, sounding less friendly than he had for Sister Mary Grace.

"Come on," Kaitlyn told her friends. "Who wants to hang around a smelly old dog?"

She started to walk away, and Sherlock, behind her back, walked several steps also, tossing his head so that his ears flopped, a good imitation of Kaitlyn's bouncing hair.

At the sound of laughter, Kaitlyn whirled around, but by then Sherlock was sitting down, looking innocently off into space.

Those children who had seen laughed even harder.

Kaitlyn assumed Amy had done or said something. "People sometimes *smell* like their dogs, too," she said.

But it was only the ones who hadn't seen Sherlock's imitation who laughed.

About half the children left with Kaitlyn. The others stayed clustered around Amy and Sherlock. *It's almost like being popular,* Amy thought—except that everybody was there because of Sherlock, not really because of her. But she proved that Kaitlyn was wrong and that Sherlock was smart by having him do tricks like rolling over and finding which backpack had Jason's cupcakes and barking answers to math questions, and that was fun.

When the bell rang and it was time for the students to gather up their things, Amy said, "Come on, Sherlock," and started toward the shady place where he was supposed to wait till school was out.

Some of the group began to follow. Amy told them, "He'll settle down faster if it's just me. Otherwise he'll want to keep on showing off."

Sherlock gave a twisting jump into the air—like an outside dog catching a Frisbee—to prove Amy's point.

Once the others were headed back toward the school and were out of hearing range, Amy turned to him. "What were you doing," she demanded, "letting yourself be seen like that? You could have gotten into serious trouble."

"You said you'd get out of school at 2:30," Sherlock explained. "But I don't have a watch."

Amy stopped and put her hands on her hips. "All that jumping up and down was to see the clock?" she asked.

"Most of it," Sherlock said, but he was already beginning to squirm. He hung his head and his tail drooped. He added, "Each time, I went to a different window so I wouldn't attract so much attention by staying around one place."

"And so you could see what was going on at each window," Amy guessed.

Sherlock squirmed even more. "Time goes slowly when you're waiting."

"I know," Amy said, unable to be truly angry: Sherlock wasn't a bad dog—he was just excited to finally be out in the world. She patted his head.

Sherlock cheered up at this sign of forgiveness. His tail whipped back and forth. "Then I saw you. And I couldn't resist wanting you to see me."

Amy patted him again. "No harm done," she said. "But now you sit or walk around this area quietly." She pointed to make sure. "From here to the fence, and no farther than that tree. Whatever you do, don't cross any streets. And don't come near the school again. Knowing what time it is doesn't make time move any faster. I'll be out when I'm out."

Sherlock gave a bark, which Amy supposed meant "OK," or "I understand," or maybe even "I don't like it," but why didn't he just say so? And why was he looking beyond her instead of at her?

Reluctantly, fearing the worst, Amy turned around.

And saw Sean Gorman standing there. With his eyes wide. And his mouth hanging open. Which pretty much killed any hope Amy might have had that he hadn't heard Sherlock speaking.

Should I tell him I was practicing ventriloquism? Amy asked herself. But you wouldn't need to be smart enough to skip the second half of fourth grade to recognize that for the dumb story it was.

Sherlock was no help at all. He started chasing his tail and pretending to be interested in studying the grass and butterflies and anything else except Sean or Amy.

Maybe, Amy hoped, if she and Sherlock acted normally enough, Sean could be convinced that he had only *thought* he'd heard the dog speaking. Now she only had to figure out what normal was in these circumstances.

Sean finally stopped staring at Sherlock. "I got him some water," he told Amy, holding out one of the plastic soup bowls from the cafeteria, "because you said he doesn't like the heat."

"Oh," Amy said, unwilling to take the bowl. Trapped by her own cleverness. "Thank you."

"How . . ." Sean said. "What . . . I . . ."

Maybe insanity runs in his family, Amy thought, and she could make him believe he'd been hearing voices.

"Yes?" she said innocently.

Sean turned back to Sherlock. "How do you do that?" he demanded. "How do you know how to talk?"

Amy fought the urge to say, "He's that new breed of Mexican Speaking Spaniel." Sean wasn't going to believe anything except the truth. She had to hope he was kind-hearted as well as smart. She said, "He's a science experiment. And the scientists are out to get him—to cut open his brain to see how it works. If you tell anybody, you could get him killed."

Sean set the bowl of water on the grass.

Sherlock approached slowly and let Sean pet him.

"I won't tell anybody," Sean assured them both.

7

NOTES

There wasn't time for much explaining. But, as Amy and Sean hurried back indoors, she admitted what she didn't dare say in front of Sherlock: "I'm worried," she told him, "that my parents might not let me keep a dog."

"What if they don't?" Sean asked. He was the shortest boy in fifth grade—he'd been one of the shortest boys in fourth grade—and he was working hard at keeping up with the taller Amy.

"I don't know," Amy admitted. "Could *you* take him?" She hated that idea. Sherlock was more than everything she could want in a pet. He was everything she could want in a friend. He was, in fact, much that she wanted to be: daring and smart—*but not too smart,* she thought, looking at Sean—and open and friendly and likable. He could be a bit more reliable, but nobody was perfect. She didn't want to give him up—even to Sean, who didn't seem half as bad as she'd first thought.

"We already have a dog," Sean said. "And my parents complain *she's* too much trouble. They'd never agree to two." He lowered his voice as they entered the school building. "We'll just have to think of a plan so your parents *have* to say yes."

She liked that much better than a plan to get *his* parents to say yes, and he went up even further in her opinion.

Inside their classroom, math had already started by the time they arrived. When they came in together, Kaitlyn whispered, loud enough for just about everybody to hear, "Isn't that cute! See, there *is* a right person for everyone. Even people like Amy and Sean."

That lessened her sense of gratitude to Sean in a hurry.

Sister Mary Grace gave Kaitlyn a stern look, but the damage was already done. People started making kissy lips at Amy. She supposed they made kissy lips at Sean, too, but she refused to look in his direction, so she couldn't be sure.

The situation didn't improve when Sarah, sitting behind her, tapped her on the shoulder and handed her a folded-up note. The note had her name on the outside, and on the inside it said:

Where do you live?

Amy turned to give Sarah a puzzled look. Sarah, looking extremely pleased with herself, nodded toward Sean, who was watching with an expectant expression that confirmed he *had* been the one to send the note.

Ignoring the grins all around her, Amy wrote her address. When Sister Mary Grace was facing the blackboard, Amy handed the note back to Sarah, who handed it to Minneh across the aisle, who handed it backward to Kaitlyn, who opened it—despite the fact that Amy had written Sean's name clearly on the outside. Kaitlyn smirked, refolded the note, and handed it across to Adam, out of whose hand Sean snatched it.

A short while later, Sarah tapped Amy again.

"What?" Amy snapped, but softly, so as not to attract Sister Mary Grace's attention.

Sarah handed her another note. This one said:

Do your parents really work?

Amy turned in her seat to give Sean a dirty look for the embarrassment he was causing with his silly questions, but she nodded to assure him that her parents really *did* work.

But Sean wasn't finished. He moved his lips in exaggerated fashion, silently mouthing another question. Amy shook her head, shrugging at the same time, and touched her ear.

Sean indicated his wristwatch.

Surely he wasn't asking what time it was: There was a clock on the front wall. Amy glanced in that direction and saw that Sister Mary Grace was watching her with upraised eyebrows.

"Some problem?" Sister Mary Grace asked.

Amy shook her head and looked hurriedly down at her desk.

Kaitlyn snickered loudly.

"Kaitlyn?" Sister Mary Grace asked. "Do *you* have a problem?"

"Not me," Kaitlyn said. "I'm just an innocent bystander."

"Yes," Sister Mary Grace said in a tone that indicated she might not be 100 percent sure of this. "Then perhaps you can work out *this* problem on the board." She held out the chalk.

Kaitlyn sighed and muttered, "Get me in trouble," as she passed Amy, but everybody knew that the truth was she loved the attention.

Times, Amy thought as Kaitlyn multiplied fractions, and suddenly connected Sean's question about time with his earlier one about her parents working. Under "Do your parents really work?" she wrote:

My mother gets home 4 - 4:30.
Father about 5:15.

She hurriedly refolded the note and on the front of it added Raymond's name, connected by an arrow to Sean's name, since people apparently didn't have the sense to pass it *around* Kaitlyn. Raymond wasn't the most likable or trustworthy person, but at least he wasn't likely to hold on to it until Kaitlyn got back from the board and then give it to her, the way Minneh was.

Amy made it through the rest of math fine, but as Sister Mary Grace was giving them their homework assignment, there came another tap on her shoulder.

This note said:

Trust me.

Amy had just barely glanced at it when Sister Mary Grace reached over and plucked it from her fingers.

Amy was torn between the desire to die right then and there, and the urge to live long enough to strangle Sean first.

Sister Mary Grace read the note, then refolded it, then put it in her pocket. "I know your dog following you to school was not intentional," she said. "But this day has been one disruption after another. *Please* settle down." The way she emphasized *please* held the hint of a last warning.

"Yes, Sister," Amy mumbled.

Sister Mary Grace turned to Kaitlyn, who had just leaned over to whisper to Ashley, "Got her that time!"

Sister Mary Grace asked, "And do you have anything to add this time, Kaitlyn?"

Kaitlyn got up, stood tall, and spoke in her best school-assembly voice. "I just want to congratulate you on a job well done. In public schools, they let kids get away with murder. I know some people say that nuns are a thing of the past, but I don't believe it for a minute." Kaitlyn nodded for emphasis and sat down again.

Sister Mary Grace paused for a good five seconds before saying, "Thank you, Kaitlyn. You don't know what a weight that takes off my mind." If she had been talking to anyone besides Kaitlyn, Amy would have suspected that maybe Sister Mary Grace was being sarcastic. But teachers all loved Kaitlyn. The other students all loved Kaitlyn, and so did everybody's parents. Amy was sure she was the only person in the world who didn't think everything Kaitlyn said or did was wonderful.

Still, even though it wasn't intentional, Kaitlyn had done Amy a good turn: Sister Mary Grace had been distracted and was letting the note-passing incident drop.

Trust me, Amy thought, turning around for a quick glare at Sean. All that had gotten her so far was trouble.

PLANS

After all the buses had pulled out of the school's parking lot, the children who lived close enough to walk home were dismissed. Most of Amy's friends were bus riders or lived in the other direction, so she usually walked home alone. She had expected that this would be especially true today, getting out late, but Sister Mary Grace canceled the detention Amy should have served for being tardy. "Just get your dog home," Sister Mary Grace said, tearing up the detention slip, "and we'll call it even."

Outside, a small crowd gathered around her—not only fifth graders, but some of the younger children, too, and even one sixth-grade boy, though he only walked one block with the group before turning down a side street. Even Minneh—Kaitlyn's shadow—was there, though Kaitlyn, of course, was not. Amy suspected that Kaitlyn had sent her to spy.

Sherlock jumped and begged and fetched and shook hands with anyone who asked, and in between he pranced by Amy's side, looking as proud of himself as though he were leading a parade. He must have checked the clocks in every room of the school, Amy thought, for just about everybody seemed to have personally seen his jumping routine.

Still, at least he remembered not to talk, even when one of the girls commanded, "Speak, Sherlock. Speak!"

Sherlock glanced at Amy for instructions.

Feeling like a fool, Amy barked, to show him what was expected.

Agreeably, Sherlock barked, too.

One of the fourth graders howled, like a wolf baying at the moon.

So did Sherlock.

Then all of the fourth graders howled.

Sherlock howled louder.

So much for sneaking home quietly, Amy thought. The neighbors had to be able to hear them from a block away.

But finally the noisy crowd arrived at her front yard, and finally—after many, many *Good-bye*s and *Good doggie*s and *See you tomorrow*s—they moved on from her front yard. And then Amy realized she had an even bigger problem: She could no longer put off worrying about what she was going to do with Sherlock. She sat down on the front step and rested her chin on her hands, her elbows on her knees.

Sherlock sat down next to her and wedged his head between her arms so that she pretty much *had* to pet him. "What's wrong?" he asked. "Is that boy going to call Animal Control? Or Dr. Boden at the college?"

Boy? Amy had to think. "You mean Sean?" She shook her head. "No, I think we can trust him." She thought about it and realized she wasn't just saying it to reassure Sherlock. "I think he's OK. I'm just trying to figure out what I should tell my parents."

"*I* can tell them," Sherlock offered. "Just like I told you."

Amy must have been making a face, because Sherlock asked, "What? What's wrong?"

"Oh, I don't know if anything is," Amy said. "It's just that sometimes parents. . . . Well, they're grown-ups."

Sherlock waited for more to this explanation. "Do you want to scratch my belly while you're thinking?" he asked. He rolled over, as though for her convenience, exposing the soft paler fur underneath.

Distracted, Amy scratched. "I mean, I don't *think* they'd call Dr. Boden. I don't *think* they'd want somebody to cut open your brain. But they might say it's none of their business. They might say you belong to the college and we don't have any right to keep you. I just can't be sure."

"Oh." Sherlock rolled back over and laid his head on his paws with a sad sigh. "You don't think they'd like me."

"Of course they'd like you," Amy said. "What's not to like?"

Sherlock gave a feeble wag of his tail.

Amy continued, "They'd *want* to be on your side. But I can just imagine them getting a letter-writing campaign going—like they did when they thought there needed to be a light at the corner, instead of just a stop sign. They went around and talked to the neighbors and got them to sign a petition and had town meetings, and they got the light, but it took about two years."

"Dr. Boden isn't going to wait two years," Sherlock said.

Amy nodded. "I know. So we can't tell them the truth. I'll tell them . . ."—she considered—". . . that you followed me home. That you're a lost dog."

"Is *lost* different from *strayed*?" Sherlock asked. "Or will they be afraid I'll bite and call Animal Control?"

Amy ignored the fact that he was right. "I'll tell them how nice and friendly you are," she said. "And smart. I'll say"—Amy let a little bit of whine creep into her voice—" 'Can't we keep him until his owners show up? We'll put up signs saying we've found him, and I promise to walk him and feed him and take care of him myself.' I'll say, 'Ever since Mom went back to work, I'm always alone and you never say *yes* to me anymore about anything.' "

Sherlock looked skeptical. "Is that likely to work?"

"It might," Amy said.

But she couldn't even convince herself.

MORE PLANS

"Are you hungry?" Amy asked. Mom didn't approve of snacks—but surely the rules were different for dogs than for people.

Sherlock nodded. "I haven't eaten since last night."

That definitely meant the rules should be different.

Amy took Sherlock into the kitchen, and she opened the refrigerator door. "What do they normally feed you?"

"Doktor Woof Dog Food." Then—he must have been reciting from memory—" 'Crunchy, veterinarian-approved, bite-sized biscuits that supply all of your dog's daily nutritional needs and prevent tartar build-up on teeth, to keep your pet's breath smelling fresh.' "

He added, "They come in a bag with a picture of a pretty cocker spaniel."

"Uh-huh," Amy said. She poked at a foil-wrapped package that might have been meat loaf, in which case her mother had prepared it the night before for tonight's dinner; or it might have been fruitcake left over from Christmas, four months ago, which hardly seemed a fair thing to inflict on Sherlock for his first meal with them. She peeked into various plastic containers and found grapes, leftover beans, corn chowder, and chopped onion. She closed the refrigerator and opened the cupboard. Not much to choose from there, either. "How about tuna fish?" she asked. "Or is that just for cats?"

Sherlock shuddered.

"You don't like tuna?" Amy asked, wondering whether he'd eat cereal, some of which at least looked like dry dog food.

"I don't like cats," Sherlock said. "Which is strange because I've never actually met one. But they *sound* terrible. Tuna is fine. Sometimes some of the students shared their lunches with me when Dr. Boden wasn't looking, and I like tuna. If it's the kind without too much mayonnaise."

"It doesn't actually come with *any* mayonnaise," Amy said. "That's added."

"Wow," Sherlock said.

Amy opened a can and dumped the tuna into a small bowl, then she set out another bowl with water. Her mother, she guessed, would consider those bowls unfit for human use if she ever suspected, so Amy would have to be sure to wash them and have them back up in the cupboard before her mother got home to see.

"This is good," Sherlock said, just as the doorbell rang.

Now who, Amy thought, trying to hide the worry from her face, *could that be?*

She must not have done a good job, for Sherlock asked—as he seemed to be doing a lot recently—"What's wrong?"

"It's too early for my mom," Amy explained. "And, anyway, she'd use her key. I'm not expecting anyone. Come on." She gestured for him to follow. "If we go to the top of the stairs, there's a window that looks out over the front stoop and we can see who it is."

She started for the stairs, but Sherlock went directly to the front door. He sniffed underneath the door. "It smells like that boy from school," he said, "Sean."

"Sean takes the bus in the other direction entirely," Amy said. But when she got to the window, she saw Sherlock was right: Sean was on the stoop, and there was a bicycle lying on the lawn, which explained how he'd gotten there.

She opened the door just as Sean was pressing the doorbell a second time.

"What are you doing here?" she demanded.

"Gee, are you that friendly to all your visitors?" Sean asked. He turned his attention from her without waiting for an answer. "Hi, Sherlock. How are you doing?"

"Fine," Sherlock said. "Did you know that tuna comes without mayonnaise?"

"Yeah," Sean said. "My dad's got high cholesterol, so everything that comes in the house lately is fat free. Dry tuna is actually better than tuna with fat-free mayonnaise."

Sherlock nodded. "Tiffany was always on a diet," he said. "So she used fat-free mayonnaise, which was the worst kind."

"Excuse me," Amy said, resentful of being ignored. "Did you bicycle all the way over here just to discuss tuna with Sherlock?"

"No," Sean said reasonably. "He was the one who brought up the subject." He went back to his bicycle and started rummaging through the pouch attached to the handlebars.

Amy followed and tried sniffing at him, discreetly. She didn't notice that Sean smelled at all, but she knew dogs had better noses than people. Sherlock probably could smell *her*, also.

Sean looked up suddenly, and Amy wondered if he'd heard her sniffing. He didn't say anything about that. He said, "I came to give you this." He held up a brown leather collar, from which a tag dangled. The tag said: BIG RED.

"It's my dog's collar," Sean explained when Amy didn't say anything. He showed her the flip side, on which were engraved Sean's name, address, and phone number. "For Sherlock."

"But," Amy pointed out, "Sherlock isn't big and he isn't red."

"I'm sorry," Sean said, sounding more annoyed than sorry, "but my dog *is*." He knelt to show Sherlock the collar. "You don't mind, do you?"

Sherlock sniffed the collar. "Girl dog?" he asked.

Sean nodded.

"She smells nice," Sherlock said, which was such an unexpected thing for him to say, it made Amy giggle. Sherlock let Sean fasten the collar around his neck. It was a little too loose, but not so much so as to be obvious.

"There we go," Sean said. "Just in time."

Amy looked up to see what he meant and saw her mother pulling into the driveway.

"I have a plan," Sean whispered. "Trust me."

Amy had already seen how far *that* had gotten her.

10
◆ ◆ ◆

CONVINCING MOM

*H*i, honey," Amy's mom said. She glanced at Sean, but didn't even seem to notice Sherlock. "Sorry I'm late, but I stopped for milk."

If she was late, it was only by about thirty seconds, but she was a natural worrier, so she always figured other people were, too.

"Uh, hi, Mom," Amy said. "This is, uh, Sean—" Before she could get out his last name, much less that she knew him from school, Sean burst into tears. Very noisy tears.

Which was as big a surprise to Amy as to her mother.

"Oh, dear," Mom said, shifting her grocery bag to

her other arm. She laid her hand on Sean's arm. "What's the matter, Sean?"

Sean buried his face in Sherlock's fur. "Sorry," he said, sniffling. "It's my dog."

For the first time, Mom glanced at Sherlock.

Sherlock, who'd been nudging Sean's shoulder as though to see what was the matter, must have realized at the same time Amy did that this had to be part of Sean's "trust me" plan. Sherlock put on an expression that was simultaneously brave and intelligent and concerned and pitiful.

"Your dog?" Mom repeated.

Sean nodded, showing his tear-streaked face. "Your daughter"—he waved vaguely in Amy's direction as though he'd just recently been told her name and had forgotten.

"Amy," Amy supplied.

". . . called," Sean continued, "when she found Big Red and realized he must be lost because he was so far from home."

Amy, who could get lost five blocks from home, hoped her mother wouldn't question this newfound geographical skill.

"Well, he's here now," Mom said, "and safe and sound. Would you like me to give you a lift home?"

Sean gave a howl that sounded to Amy as fake as the fourth graders imitating wolves. But Mom looked frantic. "What?" she asked. "*What?*"

"We're moving," Sean said. "And the new apartment doesn't allow pets. And my father said if we didn't find a home for Big Red by today, we'd just have to drop him off at the Humane Society. And my sister, Kaitlyn, she says when the Humane Society can't find homes for dogs, they kill them."

Amy knew that Sean was an only child. But she could take a good guess which Kaitlyn Sean was thinking might say such a thing. Sean finished, gasping and gulping dramatically for breaths, "And my sister says that only the puppies ever get adopted from the Humane Society. She says Big Red will be fried within the week."

"Oh," Mom said, looking distressed, "they don't 'fry' them. And besides, there are a lot of people who don't have the time or patience for little puppies, and they're especially looking for a dog that's already full grown and trained—"

"Big Red is very well trained," Sean said.

"I'm sure he is," Mom agreed.

"He always lets you know when he has to go out, and he never chews on the furniture or on anybody's stuff, and he doesn't dig in the yard, and he doesn't bark when he's left home alone, and he's friendly to people who like dogs, and he doesn't bother people who don't like dogs. He's very well behaved."

"I can see that," Mom said.

Amy figured it was time for her to jump in. "And he's smart," she said. "I saw that right away when he followed me home from school. Well behaved and smart."

"You can tell," Mom agreed, "just by looking at him."

Sherlock sat there doing his best to look irresistible.

"Sherlock," Amy commanded, "shake hands with my mother."

Sherlock offered his paw and Mom shook it.

Then Mom said, "I thought his name was Big Red."

Amy said, "Uh . . ."

Sean said, "It is. But . . ." He bit his lip, thinking.

"But I thought Sherlock fit better," Amy said. "Seeing as he isn't big. Or red." She finished lamely, "But he is smart."

"He's so smart," Sean said, "he knows when you're talking to him, no matter what you call him." He looked ready to burst into tears again. "If only I could find a good home for him."

"Hmmm," Mom said noncommittally, maybe even a bit suspiciously, despite the ingratiating way Sherlock was rolling on his back to expose his soft, white belly.

"Oh, please, Mom," Amy said.

"He's a good watchdog," Sean told Mom. "And he's loyal and trustworthy and obedient."

"Just like a Boy Scout," Mom said.

"Please," Amy begged. "Please, please. I get so lonely, home alone, waiting for you and Dad to get home from work, and sometimes it's scary."

Mom looked amazed to hear this never-before-mentioned news. She said, "He truly sounds like a wonderful dog, but I can't make a decision like that without talking it over with your father."

Dad, Amy figured, would be a pushover compared to Mom. "Could we try it," she asked, making her voice little, "if it's OK with Daddy, for a day or two? If it doesn't work out, we could always . . . you know . . . let the Humane Society kill him."

"Amy!" Mom gasped, with an anxious glance toward Sean, despite any doubts she may have had. She sighed. Loudly. Twice. Then she told Sean, "If it doesn't work out, we'll put an ad in the paper saying that he's free to a good home. No matter what, we can at least keep him that long."

"Thank you! Thank you!" Amy and Sean cried, dancing around with excitement. Sherlock gave a dog version of a happy dance.

"Hmmm," Mom said again. To Sean she added, "Well, if you don't need that ride, I'm going in to make dinner. Good luck in your new home."

It took Sean at least two seconds too long to remember. "Thanks," he said, making up in brightness what he lacked in promptness. He hugged Sherlock. "Good-bye, Big Red," he said. "I'll miss you, but I'm sure these people will grow to love you."

Sherlock licked his face and looked sad, but then he walked up to Amy's mom and wagged his tail.

"I'm sure," Mom repeated, without conviction. She went inside, but Amy and Sean and Sherlock didn't dare speak anymore.

Amy waved as Sean started pedaling down the sidewalk, until Mom must have reached the kitchen and noticed the remains of Sherlock's dinner in the family dinnerware.

"*Amy!* Get in here this minute!"

11

◇◆◇

IN THE FRONT YARD

Amy told Sherlock, "We need to have you impress my father, so that he'll let me keep you."

Sherlock sat with his tongue hanging out and eagerly asked, "Would he be impressed by the eight times table?"

"Probably too impressed," Amy said. "We decided you shouldn't talk, remember? I was thinking more like you could bring him his newspaper when he comes home from work. Dogs in movies always fetch newspapers and slippers for the father when he comes home from work."

"Always?" Sherlock asked.

"Well, except, of course, for Lassie," Amy said.

"She's too busy rescuing children who've fallen into abandoned wells to worry about stuff like fetching newspapers." Before he could ask, she added, "I don't know where there are any abandoned wells, with or without trapped children in them."

So she coached him in newspaper delivery.

As soon as Dad walked in the front door, a tail-wagging Sherlock thrust the newspaper into his hand while Amy explained—all in one breath so Dad wouldn't have a chance to say no—what a wonderful dog Sherlock was, and how overburdened the Humane Society was, and how the family didn't believe in capital punishment, and how that should certainly include innocent dogs as well as terrorists and murderers, and it was all right with Mom if it was all right with him—which wasn't exactly what Mom had said, but it was close.

"We'll see," Dad said, which Amy took as permission to tell Mom that Dad had said it was all right with him if it was all right with her.

But Dad just tossed the newspaper on the table by the front door without even looking at it, which kind of ruined the effect of Sherlock's having handed it to him. So Amy told Sherlock, "We'll try again later."

"When?" Sherlock asked.

"Soon," she told him.

But what happened soon was that midway through preparing dinner Mom yelled, "Help!" It sounded much more serious than when she simply needed an extra pair of hands.

Amy and Sherlock came dashing in from setting the dining-room table. Dad, who'd been halfway up the stairs to change out of his business clothes, ran back down.

In the kitchen, the water that was supposed to be going down the drain was instead pouring out of the pipe under the sink. Dad got under there in a hurry, despite the fact that he was still wearing his good clothes.

"Wrench!" he yelled.

Mom headed for the basement to get him one.

"Bucket!" he yelled.

Amy opened the broom closet.

"Paper!"

It was, Amy thought, a natural mistake.

How was an eager-to-please dog waiting for a signal to deliver the newspaper to know that Dad meant paper towels to mop up the spill?

Amy turned from the cupboard in time to see Sherlock come running, the newspaper between his teeth, and go into a skid on the wet kitchen floor. Toenails clicking on the tiles, he tried to backpedal. No use. He slid into Dad's back, Dad jumped and smacked his head on the bottom of the sink, and the two ends of pipe he had been holding together twisted, sending another gush of sudsy water onto him and the floor.

Amy put a finger to her lips because Sherlock looked so upset she was sure he was going to forget himself and apologize. Hurriedly, she apologized for him. "Sorry, sorry," she told Dad, handing him both a bucket and the roll of paper towels. She figured the apology would be appropriate whether he knew it was her dog who had run into him, or if he thought she was the one. He looked a little bit stunned and may well not have known what had hit him. She made a quick get-out-of-here motion with her hand, and Sherlock slunk out of the kitchen, head and tail drooping.

Eventually the sink was fixed, the mess cleaned up, dinner eaten.

The third time Sherlock gave Dad the newspaper—when Dad was sitting in the living room, looking exhausted—it worked. "Thanks," Dad told Sherlock, and patted him on the head.

Amy breathed a sigh of relief.

Still, she whispered to Sherlock, "Let's play outside," because she didn't want her parents to think they were underfoot. And because she didn't want Sherlock to be there when Dad tried to unstick the damp pages from each other.

Amy found a Frisbee in the garage in a box of summer stuff. "Here we go!" she called, tossing it across the front lawn.

Sherlock wasn't exactly a natural, but he did eventually get the hang of it. Then he found that sometimes he could have more fun if he didn't hand the Frisbee right back to Amy but made her chase him for it.

"Enough!" Amy finally said. "You've worn me out." She held her hand out for the Frisbee, but

Sherlock wouldn't give it back. He kept running around her, still holding the Frisbee in his mouth. At first Amy laughed that he was so excited he didn't want to stop, but after a few more moments she said, "Come on, now, really. It's beginning to get dark out, and chilly."

Sherlock dropped the Frisbee, but only long enough to bark at her. When she leaned to pick it up, he snatched it away and even growled at her.

"Be like that, then," she said, and took a step toward the house. Sherlock ran into her, so that she almost fell. "Sherlock!" she said.

But then he dropped the Frisbee and ran to the edge of the lawn, where he started barking and barking at someone who was approaching.

Finally Amy noticed the young woman who was walking along the sidewalk, stopping occasionally to tack some sort of flier to telephone poles.

Finally Amy caught on.

She went to stand next to Sherlock and pretended that she was there to hold on to his collar. "Someone you know?" she whispered.

Sherlock's head dipped in a nod while he continued barking.

Amy raised her voice to say, "Come on, you dumb dog!" She tugged on the collar Sean had provided them with.

The young woman with the fliers hesitated at the edge of the yard. Too young to be a professor, Amy guessed: more likely one of the college students.

"Don't worry," Amy assured her. "He's noisy and he doesn't obey, but he doesn't bite." She turned her attention back to Sherlock. "Come on, Big Red," she said, figuring *Sherlock* was obviously the name of a smart dog, and she didn't want this woman realizing he was a smart dog. "Knock it off before the neighbors complain again." Subtle hint for a clever college student that he'd been with the family for a while.

Any sensible passerby would have kept on moving, but the young woman stopped. "Hi," she said. "Your dog looks like quite a handful."

"He is," Amy told her. "He never listens."

The front door opened and Amy's dad leaned out just long enough to yell, "Amy! Control that dog of yours!"

Sherlock gave one more bark, but he didn't dare get on Dad's bad side, so he stopped.

The woman said, "I'm looking for a dog like yours."

Amy hoped her voice didn't give her away as she asked, "What? One that doesn't behave?"

The woman laughed. "No, actually the dog I'm looking for is very well behaved. But he looks just like your dog." She put her hand out and Sherlock let her set her hand on his head, but only for an instant. He backed away before she could actually pet him. The woman held out her stack of fliers. "Take one," she said.

Amy did because it would have looked suspicious

to refuse. There, under big letters saying LOST, was a picture of Sherlock.

"The dog I'm looking for belongs to the college," the woman said as Amy read about the missing dog.

Amy gave a snort of scorn. "College?" she repeated. "Big Red flunked out of obedience school."

The woman laughed again. She didn't look mean. Amy wouldn't have picked her out as someone who would murder intelligent dogs just to study their brains. "Big Red," the woman said. She moved closer again, and Sherlock let her scratch under his jaw, near where the dog tag Sean had given them dangled from the collar. Amy couldn't tell if she actually checked. "Big Red," the woman repeated, still sounding friendly, but perhaps a bit too interested. "Odd name for a small brown dog."

"He's named after someone," Amy said, the only thing she could think of.

"Oh, yes?" the woman answered in a noncommittal tone.

And, because that seemed to require something more, Amy said, "My grandfather."

The woman looked startled, but all she said was, "The dog I'm looking for answers to the name F-32. He's a very valuable animal. There'll be a reward. The phone number is on the flier."

"OK," Amy said.

The woman continued walking, occasionally stopping to fish a thumbtack out of her pocket to put fliers up on the telephone poles. Amy and Sherlock stood silently watching her, but Amy felt Sherlock tremble under her hand. The woman was too far away before Amy thought of what she should have said. She should have said, "F-32? Who's *he* named after?"

12
◇◆◇

MINNEH

*I*n school the next day, Amy didn't have a chance to talk to Sean all morning. So, as they were going into the cafeteria, she abruptly walked away from her friends, including Andrea, who was in the middle of a funny story, and she cut in line in front of Sean.

"Hey!" Sean's friend Chris complained.

"Oh, hush," Amy told him.

This was so unlike Amy, Chris hushed. And when they'd gotten their food and Amy said, "Sean and I need to talk—alone," Chris left them alone, though it was almost unheard of for fifth-grade boys and girls to sit together. Sometimes they shared a table— there were almost always boys, for example, wherever

Kaitlyn Walker sat—but even then the girls clustered at one end and the boys at the other.

But Amy directed Sean to one of the tiny tables in the corner that only sat three or four.

Several of their classmates gave them knowing looks, and the kissy lips started again.

"Here." Amy reached into her pocket to get the dog tag that said BIG RED. She also handed him a fistful of change, her entire savings, because she wasn't good at saving. "Will this be enough for you to get another collar for your dog?"

Sean shrugged. "Yeah, sure," he said in a way that made Amy suspect that collars were probably more expensive than she would have guessed. "Thanks for the tag back," Sean said. "My parents haven't noticed yet about the collar being gone, but with the tag, I can get a new collar at the mall and just say I thought it was time for a different one. Good thinking."

Amy refused to take credit where it wasn't due. "No," she admitted, "I haven't been thinking well." She leaned in closer. "Some girl, a student from the college, was putting up fliers in our neighborhood, and there I was in the front yard playing with Sherlock, for all the world to see."

Sean waved away someone who looked ready to come sit with them. He lowered his voice. "Did she recognize him?"

"Sherlock isn't sure." Amy lowered her voice, too. "He said that this girl—her name is Rachel—was one of the nicest ones there, but I figure she can't be all that nice if she's helping this Dr. Boden track him down."

"Maybe Dr. Boden has made it a class requirement," Sean said. "You know: 'If you want to pass, hand out these fliers . . .' "

Amy liked that Sean seemed willing to believe the best about people. Still, she shrugged. "Anyway, she kept saying how much Sherlock looked like the dog she was searching for, and then right before she left, she goes like this to him"—Amy gestured to show scratching under a dog's chin—"which apparently is something Sherlock likes. Sherlock says he tried not to wag his tail, but even from where I was standing, I could tell he liked it. The thing is, we don't know if this Rachel does that to all dogs."

"Lots of dogs like it," Sean said, "so lots of people do it."

It was a little reassuring. A very little. "Anyway," Amy continued, "I spent the rest of the night listening for the doorbell to ring. I kept waiting for her to show up with the professor—or the police—to demand the college's property back. Of course, my parents wouldn't know not to admit we'd only had the dog since that afternoon, and they'd be sure to blab all about the poor little boy"—she gestured to Sean and came close to knocking over her milk carton—"whose family was moving into an apartment that wouldn't allow pets. That's when I thought about the dog tag. Dr. Boden would demand to call the phone number on it. And—unless we were lucky enough that you were the one to answer the phone—your parents would say that they weren't moving, and that your dog was right there with them, except that somehow her collar and tags were missing. So I figured I'd say that I threw the tag away at school. I don't think anybody—even a determined scientist like Dr. Boden—would go through all the garbage Dumpsters here searching for one tiny piece of metal no bigger than a quarter."

"Hard to know for sure," Sean said. He didn't put her on the spot by asking what she'd say if anyone asked *why* she'd taken the tag to school to throw it out. In his heart, she guessed, he too must suspect that if Dr. Boden saw Sherlock, he wouldn't believe her story for a moment, no matter what.

Sean tried to shoo away someone else who was approaching their table, but this person wouldn't be put off.

Minneh Tannen pretended not to see Sean and looked at Amy.

Across the room, one of the boys at Kaitlyn's table called out in a singsong rhyme:

"Minneh, Minneh!
Take your tray,
and go away!"

This was followed by loud laughter, as though the silly rhyme was something clever.

"May I sit with you?" Minneh asked in such a

little voice that Amy went ahead and nodded, even though she and Sean had more to talk about. Minneh put her tray down, then sat quietly for a moment, not saying anything and not looking at either of them. Finally, staring down at her food, she said, "Kaitlyn said I couldn't sit at her table."

Of course Kaitlyn had more people wanting to sit at her table than there could ever be room for, but Minneh was one of the regulars, one of—Amy had thought—Kaitlyn's best friends.

Sean, being a boy and not having the sense to be polite, asked the question Amy was dying to ask: "How come?"

"Because I walked home with Amy yesterday."

Amy remembered Minneh had been there but waited for her to explain more.

Minneh stared at a spot between Amy and Sean. "See, I live on Ravenwood Terrace, which runs between Thurston Road and Genesee Park Boulevard, so I can walk home on either street, except that I always go on the boulevard, with Kaitlyn. But yesterday Amy had all those people with her, laughing and having fun with her dog doing tricks and everything, and I said to Kaitlyn that for just this once I thought I'd walk down Thurston. Just to be sure, I even asked if that was OK."

She asked for permission? Amy thought in wonder.

"And Kaitlyn said"—Minneh tossed her head—" 'Do what you think is best.' Which I thought meant she didn't mind." Minneh went back to staring down at her food. "But this morning she wouldn't talk to me at all, and when I went to take my usual seat, she said . . ."

Amy leaned closer. "She said . . ." she prompted, as tactless as Sean because she was dying to know.

Minneh mumbled, " 'Nobody here wants your company. Go see if the lovebirds are willing to take you.' " She looked up at Amy and Sean quickly, as though afraid she'd offended them by repeating this. "I was so afraid you'd say I couldn't sit here, and then I wouldn't have known what to do. Everybody was watching, sure you'd tell me to go away, and then there I'd be, holding my lunch, and no place to sit down."

Amy saw that Kaitlyn and her crowd *were* watching, ready to laugh. "We *did* have a good time yesterday, didn't we?" Amy said. "With those fourth graders howling?"

A bubble of laughter burst from Minneh. She quickly put her hands over her mouth.

"Howling?" Sean asked.

"You know," Amy said. She demonstrated, whisper fashion.

People at the surrounding tables turned to look.

Minneh covered her mouth again, for people in Kaitlyn's crowd always wanted to appear at their sophisticated best. But her eyes sparkled with amusement.

"That's not a howl," Sean said. "That's a pathetic little yodel." He threw his head back and *howled*.

Everyone turned to look.

Minneh joined in, hesitantly, unsure at first, then louder.

Why not? Amy thought, and howled along with them until Sister Mary Grace came over and asked, "Is that absolutely necessary?"

They stopped howling, but found other things to laugh about until—how could the half hour have gone by so quickly?—the bell rang and they had to scramble to clear the table.

13
◇◇◇

BEING WATCHED

I can't ever remember laughing so much," Minneh told Amy as the fifth-grade classes filed outside to the playground.

"Nonsense," Amy said. "Kaitlyn and her crowd are always laughing."

Minneh became thoughtful. "Yeah, well," she said slowly, "with Kaitlyn, we're always laughing *at* other people. You know, Kaitlyn can be hysterically funny—if you're not the one she's poking fun at."

"Hmm," Amy said. *Is that why she's so popular?* she wondered. *Do people always want to be around her just to lessen the chance that they'll be the one she's laughing at?*

Minneh finished, "But you're not so much funny, as fun."

Amy didn't know what to say, but she was pleased. Until Sherlock, she hadn't thought of herself as a fun person. She didn't have long to wonder about what Minneh had said, however, for as soon as she stepped out the door, she saw that Sherlock was in the playground, waiting for her.

Now what? He had agreed the safest thing for him was to wait at home. She wanted to be angry with him for not following instructions, because being angry meant she wouldn't have to worry that something had gone wrong. But the suspicion nagged at her that he was too smart to lightly risk coming out when he knew there were dangerous people looking for him.

She tried to interpret his body language. His tail drooped but was wagging, slightly. It might mean he knew he had done something wrong and he was hoping she wouldn't be annoyed at his disobeying her. Or it might mean he was trying to act normally in front of the other children until he could get her alone to tell her about some catastrophe.

The closer she got to him, the more convinced she became that something bad had happened.

"Sherlock," she said in the tone she used when there were others around—the tone that said, "I may be talking to this dog, but I don't really expect him to answer." She stooped down to give him a hug. "You naughty dog. Why aren't you back home?" She hugged him again because he looked upset about something—she had no idea what—and she wanted to make sure he didn't forget himself and tell her.

"Come on, boy," she said, trying to lead him back to the shady corner where she had left him yesterday.

But Sherlock wouldn't follow, and when she tugged on his collar, he dug all four feet into the dirt, unwilling to go there.

Amy trusted his intelligence enough not to insist. "Well, where should we go?" she asked.

Sherlock headed for the other end of the playground.

Several of the children started to follow, including Minneh. "Could we be alone?" Amy said. There was no way she could think of to make an exception for Sean. "I need to yell at him, and he gets embarrassed if I do that in front of people."

Most of the children laughed, but agreeably, and they drifted away. But Kaitlyn called out, "Psycho."

And there were still those who laughed nastily at that and repeated it.

"Sherlock," Amy said quietly as they walked, "you can't keep following me to school. I convinced Mom that you'd be better off in the backyard than locked up in the basement, but if Sister Mary Grace sees you and calls home to complain, Mom *will* put you in the basement because she doesn't know you well enough to trust you upstairs all by yourself yet. The basement will be boring." Amy stooped down to lessen the chance of being overheard. She saw he was shaking, as he had when the college student, Rachel, had been speaking with them. "What's wrong?" Amy asked. "What happened?"

"Do you see across the street?" Sherlock asked.

Amy figured he meant near where he had originally refused to go. She looked and saw a young man there, leaning against the fence. He was smoking a cigarette and looking around as though he just happened to be there, just happened to be enjoying a fine spring day, but Amy saw the way his gaze kept returning to Sherlock. And her. "Dr. Boden?" she asked.

"Ed," Sherlock answered. "Another of the students. He came almost as soon as your parents left for work. He stood by the fence and kept calling me. I barked a bit, but I didn't want the neighbors complaining. So then I went over and sniffed him, as though I was an outside dog who had never smelled him before." Sherlock hung his head. "I even considered biting. But I couldn't bring myself to do it."

Amy squeezed him tightly, loving him for being so true to his gentle nature, even when he was in danger.

Sherlock continued, "He kept saying, 'Come on, F-32, don't you recognize me?' I tried to act bored, like I didn't understand him, and I walked into my water bowl so that it tipped over, and I dug in your garden a bit—I hope your parents don't get too upset—but mostly I pretended to sleep, because I wasn't sure what a regular outside dog would do."

Amy patted his head to reassure him, "We'll have to ask Sean," she said. "*I* don't know how most dogs spend their days, either."

"Then," Sherlock continued, "finally he went away, and I thought, *What if he's gone to get Dr. Boden?* I came to ask you what to do, but he hadn't left after all: He'd gone into his car so I couldn't smell him anymore. And he followed me here." Sherlock hung his head. "Which shows I'm not as smart as I thought."

"There's a difference between being smart and being tricky," Amy said.

Still Sherlock wouldn't raise his head. "Then tricky must be better."

"Tricky is useful," Amy admitted. "But smart is better."

Sherlock finally looked at her again. "Really?"

"Really," Amy assured him. She gave him a tight hug. "And smart and nice is best of all."

"Like you," Sherlock said.

"Yeah, right," Amy scoffed.

"Like you," Sherlock repeated, and he licked her face.

"Thank you," Amy said. First Minneh called her fun, then Sherlock called her smart and nice. She hadn't been any of those things before Sherlock. Had she? Suddenly she had an awful thought. "You didn't unlatch the gate, did you?" An ordinary dog would never be able to figure it out, but she was sure Sherlock could have gotten it in seconds.

Sherlock shook his head, his big ears flapping. "I jumped over the fence, so if Ed did bring Dr. Boden back, they wouldn't see that the latch was undone."

"Good boy," Amy said, ruffling his fur. "Clever dog."

From behind, she heard Sean speaking loudly—

probably to warn her that someone was coming. "Go away," he said. "Stop following me. Didn't you hear her say she wanted to be alone?"

Amy turned as Minneh answered, "She's my friend, too. If there's some sort of trouble, I want to help. I don't know why you're being so obnoxious all of a sudden."

Sean looked frantic, but Amy motioned for both of them to stop arguing and come closer. Sean stooped down to offer Sherlock a friendly pat, and Minneh crouched beside him.

"What's going on?" Minneh asked, instinctively knowing to whisper.

"You're never going to believe this," Amy said, "but do you see that man over there? He's bothering my dog."

Sean probably had a good idea what she was talking about. Minneh took her on faith. "Well," Minneh said, "I know how to get rid of him."

"You do?" Amy said. "How?"

"Young guy like that?" Minneh said. "Hanging around a school yard? All we have to do is tell Sister Mary Grace he's watching us and it's giving us the creeps." Minneh glared at him across the length of the playground. "He *is* giving me the creeps."

Sean said, "You mean like hint that maybe he's selling drugs? Have the police called in to arrest him?"

"No," Amy said. "If we accuse him of anything specific, then he'd know for sure."

"*Know* what?" Minneh asked.

Amy said, "He wants to take Sherlock."

"Some nerve!" Minneh sent her high-powered glare his way again. "Tell the police *that*."

"I can't," Amy admitted. "Sherlock's not really my dog."

"You're a dognapper?" Minneh asked, sounding shocked but impressed.

"She's a dog rescuer," Sean corrected.

Sherlock barked in agreement.

"Minneh," Amy asked, "is there any way you can take Sherlock home with you? This guy and his friends know where I live. If you could hide him for a couple days, just until they decide Sherlock's not coming back to my place . . ."

"I don't know," Minneh said. "My father's allergic to dogs." She snapped her fingers. "But he could hide out in our garage."

Amy's eyes filled with tears of anger and frustration at this decision being forced on her. She could see that Sherlock was afraid. Yet he was waiting for her. Trusting her. But she didn't know what to do— not for sure. What if she chose wrong? Still she tried to sound sure, so Sherlock wouldn't worry. "You hear that, Sherlock?" she said. "We'll get rid of Ed. This afternoon, you go home with Minneh. She only lives a couple blocks from us, but you'll be safer there. You be a good dog for her now." She put her finger to her lips, to warn him not to speak in front of Minneh. The fewer people who knew, the better.

Sherlock barked and nodded his head in agreement.

Minneh shook her head in amazement. "That is one smart dog," she said.

"Yes, he is," Amy said. "Now, I've got to find Sister Mary Grace . . ."

LIES

"A my," Sister Mary Grace said, "are you sure you haven't been watching too much television?"

"No, Sister," Amy said, trying to sound earnest and scared rather than nervous and guilty. If Sister Mary Grace decided to demand details and proof, Amy wasn't sure how she'd convince her—without actually accusing the young man by the fence of *doing* anything—that he was creepy.

But Sister Mary Grace put aside the papers she was grading and went with her to the back door for a look.

There were Minneh and Sean, playing catch the stick with Sherlock, and there was the young man, glancing obviously and repeatedly in their direction.

Of course, Sister Mary Grace had no reason to suspect that it was the dog that held his attention. She probably didn't even *see* the dog.

Recess came to an abrupt end with the arrival of the police, who at least did not come with lights and sirens and squealing tires.

Sister Mary Grace gave the class her old "stranger danger" lecture, which they hadn't had in at least a month. Then Sister Pat, the principal, came in and—as she usually did only once a year—gave her version of the same thing. And then Father Matt . . . By the end of the afternoon, the children had glazed eyes and slack jaws, too exhausted from the flow of words even to fidget.

Amy could have gotten through the afternoon more easily if she'd had something besides stranger danger to occupy her mind: A good hard math test would have been nice—though she guessed this was the only time in her life she would think so. As it was, all she could think about was that she had to give up Sherlock.

She tried to convince herself that it was just for a few days, but again and again she came back to the thought that Ed had been at the house, and he'd followed Sherlock here. If the people from the college had any sense at all, they'd know the dog they'd been watching was the one they wanted; they'd know Amy had been the one who'd turned Ed in to the police.

Not only might Sherlock never be able to come back from Minneh's—there was a chance even Minneh's was not safe.

She didn't know why he'd chosen her when he needed to ask for help. Maybe she'd been the first person he'd seen that morning. Maybe—being a kid—she was closer to his size than anybody else he'd seen.

Whatever the reason, he had come to her for help, and she'd barely been able to give him one day. If she'd been smarter or braver, she'd have been able to keep him safe. Regardless of what Sherlock said about her being smart, she was convinced that if she'd been the dog and Sherlock the person, he'd have done a better job of protecting her.

Feeling sorry for both him and herself, she was barely able to keep from crying until she got home.

She was still crying when her mother got home from work.

"Oh, darling," Mom said, "what's the matter?"

"Sherlock's gone," Amy said. She wasn't used to lying and didn't feel comfortable doing it—especially to her mother—so she stayed as close to the truth as she could. "He must have jumped the fence."

"Oh, dear." Mom looked around the living room in frustration. Mom took problems personally, and one of her favorite phrases was "Let's brainstorm for solutions." Her eyes brightened. "Did you write down the phone number of that boy?" she asked. "The former owner? I bet I know what happened: The dog didn't understand. I bet he ran away to be back with his old family. That happens a lot when people move, you know—the animal travels hundreds of miles and shows up at the old house."

Amy shook her head. This required a direct lie.

"When I called him yesterday, I didn't write the number down. I just dialed it directly from the dog tag."

Mom considered some more. "Now where did that tag say he lived? Beahan Road? Hinchey? Wasn't it somewhere beyond the airport?"

"I don't know," Amy said.

"They'll call us," Mom assured her. "Or, more likely, just bring the dog over." Mom had yet to settle on whether to call him Sherlock, which Amy did, or Big Red, which was what his tag said. "What was that boy's name—Sean? Sean knows the way. Sean's family will bring the dog over." She bit her lip. "Unless they moved already. But if they did, surely at least one of their old neighbors knows their new address and will contact them and let them know that their dog is wandering around their old neighborhood. *Then* they'll pick up the dog and bring him back." Mom nodded to convince herself and Amy. "From now on, we'll keep him in the house, only letting him out for walks on a leash, until he's used to us, until he realizes this is his new home." Mom hugged her and said, "Everything will work out, honey. You'll see."

The fact was none of this brainstorming had anything to do with the real problem, and Amy couldn't tell her mother so.

"Or," Mom suggested, "we could ask our neighbors if they noticed anything unusual today."

Like the unfortunate Ed hanging around all morning?

"Oh," Amy said, "that's not very likely."

But Mom with a possible solution was not to be denied. She left a note for Dad that dinner was delayed and marched next door to ask Mrs. Heintzman if she'd seen anything of their new dog.

Mrs. Heintzman hadn't. And neither had Mr. or Mrs. Griggs, nor any of the Rodriguez family, which included three generations, and at least a half-dozen children.

It was only on their way to the fourth house on their street that Mom noticed one of the fliers on a telephone pole. "Looks like this could be our dog's brother," Mom snorted. "Must be spring fever getting into all of them." She took the flier down, to be able to show people, to be able to say, "He looks something like this, but brighter eyed and more attractive."

Nobody had seen anything, and eventually even Mom had to give up. "If we don't hear anything from Sean's family by tomorrow night," Mom assured Amy, "we'll put up our own fliers."

Mom was so sure they'd be hearing from Sean's family, she got Amy fidgety, even though Amy knew better. When the phone rang at about eight, she almost knocked Dad over to get to it.

"Amy?" it was a whispered voice, with a lot of crackling going on in the background.

"Minneh?" Amy asked.

"I'm in the hall closet with the cordless phone," Minneh explained, "so my family can't hear. I just wanted to say everything's fine. Sherlock's in our garage. No sign of evil dognappers." She giggled. "Or perverts or drug dealers. I left the window open on my dad's pickup, so Sherlock could sleep on the seat instead of the hard cement floor. And I slipped him some leftover pizza for dinner, and he seemed to like it. He's a neat dog, Amy. He licked my face to thank me and everything. I'll take care of him for you. Gotta go—that's my brother pounding on the door. I guess he's expecting a call from his girlfriend. See you tomorrow."

"See you," Amy said, the first chance Minneh gave her to say anything.

Dad looked her way as she hung the phone back up. "The elusive Sean?" he asked.

"No. Minneh, from school."

"Ah," he said. "I was hoping it was good news."

It had been, in a way, but she couldn't tell him so. At least Sherlock was safe for the moment and being taken care of.

Except that the next moment the doorbell rang. And when Mom opened the door, Amy heard a man's voice announce, "I'm Dr. Franklin Boden from the college, and I'm here to speak to you about my dog."

15

◇◇◇

QUESTIONS

Amy walked quietly to the end of the living room, where she could see the entryway and the front door. Her father didn't get up from his chair, where he'd been reading the newspaper, but he pulled his reading glasses closer to the tip of his nose so that he could see over them to look at their visitor, too.

"Your dog?" Mom repeated. There was a certain tension in her voice, just a hint. Amy caught it, and Dad probably did, too; Dr. Boden wouldn't have—even though he was the cause of it: He'd gone ahead and opened the screen door without being invited, which practically put him into the house. He even had one foot up on the doorjamb, as though ready to dash in, which was obviously much too pushy for Mom. She was giving him the benefit of the doubt for now, but she was holding on to the heavier wooden door, looking ready to sweep him away with a good hard slam at a moment's notice. Behind Amy, Dad set down his newspaper and glasses and stood.

Dr. Boden said, "I think you have my dog." His tone said: *You're liars and thieves—but you've been caught so don't try to deny it*. He didn't look that much older than a college student, a rather too short, too thin man with so much nervous energy he couldn't seem to stand still. *And*, Amy thought, *way too much self-confidence*. Or maybe not enough: Maybe, like some of the high schoolers she'd seen, he was just too interested in proving himself. She didn't have any trouble believing he was the kind of person who would cut open a dog's brain to see how it worked.

And Mom looked fed up with him already, too.

Amy's father stepped in to take Mom's place guarding the door. "What makes you think we have your dog?" he asked.

"Oh, I'm sure it's just an honest mistake." Dr. Boden flashed a smile with teeth so straight and perfect they looked like they were from a denture cream commercial. The smile said: *Yeah, right*. "Apparently you missed seeing these that I distributed in the neighborhood." He held up a flier like the one Rachel had given Amy the evening before, snapping it with a flourish that said: *Fat chance*. By the light over the stoop, Amy could see that his fingernails were ragged and the skin around them raw. They looked so nasty, she resolved never to bite her fingernails again.

Dad took the flier, which Dr. Boden had practically shoved into his face. Dr. Boden himself was practically shoved into Dad's face, but Dad wouldn't retreat because—the way Dr. Boden was acting—he clearly might take that as an invitation to step right into the house. "Different dog," Dad said.

"I think not," Dr. Boden answered. "I've been talking with your neighbors, and they tell me you seem to have acquired a dog at just about the same time I lost one." Again he smiled: *Caught you*. Did he think he was so much more clever than they that he was fooling them and reassuring them?

"Different dog," Dad said more emphatically. "We know where ours came from: It belonged to a boy whose family was moving."

The smile wavered. "*If* you got it from a boy and that's what the boy said, then the boy lied. You know how children are." He made a point of looking at Amy.

She hadn't realized he had seen her there, and she shrank back.

"For example," he continued, "there was an incident this afternoon—"

Dad interrupted by trying to hand him back the flier.

Dr. Boden wouldn't take it. "Why not just let me see the dog," he said, "and I can prove it's mine by the identifying tattoo on the inside of its left ear."

Ouch, Amy said to herself at the thought of such

a tattoo. Sherlock's ears were so floppy, she hadn't noticed; but she remembered how he hadn't let Rachel pet his head. He had known she'd look and be able to identify him. Clever, clever dog. Amy wanted to kick Dr. Boden's knee and yell, *How'd you like your ears tattooed? And Sherlock is a he. Not an it, a HE*.

"As a matter of fact," Dad said, matching Dr. Boden smile for smile, "*our* dog has gone missing, too."

Dr. Boden looked exasperated. His expression said: *Can't you even come up with a good lie?* He glanced beyond Dad and Mom and Amy, into the house, as though weighing his chances of forcing his way in.

Dad started to close the door, and Dr. Boden shoved his foot in the way. "It's a very valuable animal," Dr. Boden said. "It's not some common-medical-experiment disposable mutt. I could have you up on charges of grand larceny."

"I could have you up on charges of trespassing and harassment," Dad countered.

Dr. Boden snorted. But he moved his foot out of the way.

Dad slammed the door shut.

From the window, they watched him walk around to the side of the house to look over their fence. Mom clutched at Dad's arm and glanced at the phone, but there wasn't time to call for help. As soon as Dr. Boden saw there was no dog in their yard, he went back out to the street where his car was parked. When he opened the door and the overhead light came on, Amy caught the cold glint of a metal cage in the back. Dr. Boden took out a notebook and wrote something down. Only then did he close the door and drive away.

Mom rubbed her arms as though she were chilled. "What an unpleasant man."

Dad hugged her. He hugged Amy, too. Then, crumpling the flier and throwing it away without even putting on his glasses to look at it, he said, "I hope he never gets his dog back."

"Me, too," Amy whispered. "Me, too."

16

✦ ✦

SPECIAL DAY

my knew it would be too dangerous to walk to school by way of Minneh's house: If Dr. Boden or one of his people was watching Amy, she'd lead him straight to Sherlock. Still, she planned to leave the house as early as she could get away with—in the hope that Minneh would do the same—and at least that would give them a few minutes to talk together before classes started.

But as Amy was heading for the door, Mom said, "Hold on. Don't forget me."

For a moment Amy thought Mom must still be nervous about Dr. Boden's visit last night, and suddenly *she* worried, too. Would he come looking for her at school? But then she remembered that this was a special day: This was the last day—actually, *half* day—before Easter vacation. Sister Mary Grace had invited parents to come to school because Kaitlyn Walker's grandmother was going to demonstrate how to make Ukrainian Easter eggs. After the presentation, children and parents would have a chance to decorate their own eggs.

"Oh," Amy said, trying not to sound disappointed, trying to sound, in fact, pleased. "That's right. I forgot." She watched the minutes pass as her mother finished getting ready, then, together, they traveled by car the three blocks Amy normally walked alone.

Since school was being dismissed after morning classes, Sister Mary Grace had gotten permission to use the cafeteria, where the long tables would give people enough room to work without being cramped with one or two adults plus a child to a desk. Then, after making the Easter eggs, there'd be a pizza party.

As Amy and Mom walked down the long hall to the cafeteria, Amy saw with horror that she and her mother had arrived right behind Sean Gorman and his mother. Amy and Sean had pretended in front of Mom that they hadn't known each other. How could they ever answer if she started asking complicated questions now?

Calm down, Amy told herself. *How likely is it that Mom will recognize Sean?*

She watched the back of his head and his distinctive bouncy walk.

Very likely, she decided.

"Hey, Mom," she said, practically steering her mother into the wall, "did you see these cute pictures the third graders made out of cotton balls? Aren't they fun?"

Her voice and enthusiasm must have carried, because ahead of them Mrs. Gorman also paused to look at the pictures hanging on the wall.

Mom, looking at the wall of pictures, was just starting to say, "Oh, yes, they are—" when Amy jabbed her finger at one of the pictures, demanding Mom's closer attention. "Look at the detail on this one." Out of the corner of her eye, she saw Sean notice them. It must have sunk in for him that he and Amy might have a lot of fast explaining to do because he started tugging on his mother's arm to get her moving again.

Mom was just saying, "They're—" when Amy pointed to the next picture to make sure she didn't look up, and said, "And see how this guy got bits of fluff stuck to everything."

"Yes," Mom said, "very—"

But by then Sean and his mother had turned the corner into the cafeteria, and Amy dragged on her mother's arm. "Come on," Amy said. "Hurry up or we won't get a good seat." What she meant was *Or we might have to sit too near to the Gormans*.

As soon as they stepped into the cafeteria, Amy said, "Oh, look! There's Sister Mary Grace. Do you know Sister Mary Grace?"

Mom turned in the direction Amy pointed— which happened to be at the front of the room rather than farther back, where Sean and his mother were taking seats at one of the tables. Mom started to say something—probably that of course she knew Sister Mary Grace after one Open House, two parent-teacher conferences, and bingo the first Thursday of every month—but by then Amy had spotted empty seats two tables away from Sean. "Oh, there's my best friend, Minneh," she squealed. "We've *got* to sit with her."

"Minneh?" Mom repeated quizzically. "I don't remember you ever mentioning a Minneh."

"Of course you do," Amy insisted. Once more she began tugging on her mother's arm.

Her mother hung back and whispered, "Which is Minneh? The one sitting next to that strange man who keeps sniffling and scratching himself?"

"Yes," Amy said. She called out, before Mom could suggest sitting someplace else, "Hi, Minneh. Isn't this going to be fun? This is my mom. Mom, Minneh."

"Hi, Mrs. Prochenko," Minneh said. "This is my dad."

Mr. Tannen half stood up and extended his arm as though to shake hands with Mom, but then he jerked his hand away to cover his nose and mouth as he gave a huge sneeze. "Sorry," he said. "But don't worry: I'm not contagious. This started too fast to be a cold. It's got to be allergies." He pulled his sleeve back to reveal where he'd been scratching. "Rash," he said, in case they missed the pinkish welts. "Definitely allergies. Not sure to what, though."

Mom didn't look quite ready to believe him. She obviously was worried about sitting too near, but Amy plunked herself down next to Minneh, hoping that Mom would be too polite to demand that they move.

Sister Mary Grace stepped forward, which the children recognized as a signal for quiet, but the parents didn't. "Hello, everyone," she said. She had to repeat it twice more before all the adults settled down. "I realize some of you have taken time off work to be here with us today, and I just wanted to assure you that the lesson ends promptly at 11:45, though we hope you'll stay for pizza. I'd also like to thank all of you for coming and showing support for your children and interest in their education."

Amy wasn't sure what decorating Easter eggs had to do with education, but at least it was a day without a spelling quiz.

"Everyone," Sister Mary Grace said, "I'd like you to greet Mrs. Oksanna Pudlyk, our own Kaitlyn's grandmother, who has graciously offered to demonstrate the making of traditional Ukrainian Easter eggs."

People clapped politely as Mrs. Pudlyk stood and moved to the front of the room.

Most of the children had only one parent—or grandparent, or aunt or uncle—with them, although a few had two. Kaitlyn, Amy noted, had brought not only her grandmother *and* her grandfather, but both parents. Amy wondered if Sister Mary Grace would make Kaitlyn share with Raymond Young, who had come without any adult. But Sister Mary Grace herself went to sit with Raymond, and left the Walker-Pudlyk tribe together, grinning proudly.

Mr. Tannen, who had been blowing his nose

loudly during Sister Mary Grace's announcement, leaned over Minneh and Amy to whisper to Amy's mom, "Do you know how long this is supposed to take? My boss has given me the time off, but the sooner I can get back, the better."

"Until 11:45," Mom whispered, looking embarrassed. Mr. Tannen's voice was probably a bit louder than he realized, and Mom was obviously worried that people might think they were together just because he was talking to her. She sat forward in her seat to indicate to Kaitlyn's grandmother that she, for one, was eager to learn all that Mrs. Pudlyk had to teach, however long it took.

Amy was more sympathetic to Mr. Tannen.

Mrs. Pudlyk smiled at the group and began telling the history of eggs. "The egg," she said, "it is the object of the reverence and mystery throughout the world . . ."

17

◇◇◇

EGGS AND LIES

In the Prochenko household, Mom bought Easter-egg-dye tablets to dissolve in water and vinegar—except, of course, when she forgot, leaving Amy to use liquid food color, which was messier. Amy would dunk hard-boiled eggs in the different dyes, sometimes mixing dyes in an attempt to get exciting new designer colors, though this usually resulted in something along the lines of murky brown. And sometimes she would dye half an egg one color and the other half a different color, but this always left an uneven border alternating white and overlapping colors. Frequently the overlapping colors also came out brown. After she'd finished dying the eggs, Amy would place them back in the egg carton to dry, where the dye generally accumulated at the bottom, resulting in drip streaks and a crusty tip that was two shades darker than the rest of the egg.

Ukrainian Easter eggs were nothing like that.

"First of all," Mrs. Pudlyk said with her slight Ukrainian accent—which was just difficult enough for Amy to understand that she had to concentrate on every word—"they are the works of art: The last thing you would want would be for the egg to be spoiling so that you would have to throw the egg away after working so hard to be making it so beautiful. Therefore the true Ukrainian Easter eggs is the hollow shells with the insides blown out through the pinprick holes. But I have asked Sister Mary Grace to provide the regular hard-boiled eggs because they will be easier to work with for beginners and because"— she made an airy gesture—"nobody's first attempts are the masterpieces."

Mrs. Pudlyk, whose eggs were sold at craft fairs, passed around a photo album that showed some of the eggs she had made. On the first page, she pointed out, were pictures of eggs her own grandmother had made—eggs still treasured in the family after seventy years. The last page had eggs Kaitlyn had made. Amy wanted to hate them, but they were beautiful, with tiny intricate designs drawn with, obviously, a good deal of talent and patience.

Next, Mrs. Pudlyk passed out sheets of paper on which were drawn traditional symbols and what they meant. For example, a design that went around the egg like a ribbon or border meant eternity or everlasting life; triangles made up of tiny diamond shapes were the Holy Trinity; and dots could be teardrops—or, if there were a lot of them, the stars of heaven. Birds were for wishes coming true, deer for health, roses for everlasting love. All of the designs were tiny, and the entire surface of the egg was supposed to be filled.

At the bottom of this sheet, Mrs. Pudlyk had drawn egg-shaped spaces for people to plan out and practice what they wanted to draw on their own eggs. Minneh quickly filled in one of her spaces with a smiley face, then gave it floppy dog ears—a symbol, Amy assumed, that Sherlock was well. She gave Minneh a grateful grin.

The basic idea of the eggs was to lightly draw a design in pencil, then dye repeatedly, going from lighter colors to darker, and covering over the parts that already had enough color with hot wax. The lit candles from which the wax came, Amy reasoned, were probably the single biggest reason Sister Mary Grace had invited adults: to help keep an eye on the kids so that they would be less likely to burn themselves or set the building on fire.

Mrs. Pudlyk went from table to table, lighting the candles with a device like a long, skinny lighter.

As soon as she lit theirs, Mr. Tannen sneezed and blew it out.

"Oop-la!" Mrs. Pudlyk said as she came back to relight it. "One of us has the springtime cold."

"Allergies," Mr. Tannen said, blowing his nose.

Sister Mary Grace had provided everyone with two extra eggs each, just in case of accidents. Since there would only be time to decorate one complex Ukrainian-style egg, she also provided regular dyes— and stickers, glitter, felt, and pastel-colored feathers— for people whose first eggs came out right and wanted to decorate their spare eggs.

Jennifer's grandfather promptly dropped the container of glitter.

While people scrambled to scoop the glitter up, which seemed to spread it farther and farther across the floor, somebody—Amy thought it was Jason's father—went ahead and opened the bag of feathers ahead of time. Suddenly there were feathers all over, too.

Mr. Tannen sneezed, blowing out the candle once more and sending the design sheet from which Mom was trying to copy skittering to the floor. "Sorry," he said. "Must be those feathers that I'm having an allergic reaction to. I have really bad allergies."

"Must be," Mom said. As she leaned to pick up the paper, she added in a mutter half under her breath, ". . . if they could affect you since before the bag was even opened."

Amy didn't think Mr. Tannen had heard—he was too busy summoning Mrs. Pudlyk to tell her that they needed her lighter again—but she glanced at Minneh with an apologetic grimace.

Minneh shrugged and plucked a long white dog hair off her father's sleeve while he was distracted with getting out his handkerchief.

Amy wondered if Sister Mary Grace was having second thoughts about inviting the adults. They were not as well behaved as the children, and they kept laughing and chatting with one another, and going ahead of Mrs. Pudlyk's directions so that they got things wrong, and making silly designs—which did not amuse Mrs. Pudlyk, who took Easter egg making very seriously.

Mr. Tannen sneezed out the candle a third time, and Mrs. Pudlyk sighed loudly before coming back to relight it.

Amy continued to work on her design: Sherlock, surrounded by flowers, bordered by a wreath.

"Hsst," Mom whispered. "Amy."

Amy worried that Mom was about to make another rude comment regarding Minneh's dad, but when she turned, she saw that Mom was motioning her to move out of the way. Amy followed the direction of her gaze: beyond Amy, beyond Minneh, beyond Mr. Tannen, past two tables . . .

"I can't get this," Amy said, slamming down her pencil. "Mom, can you help me draw that feather-wreath pattern?"

Mom continued to look beyond her. "Isn't that Sean?" she asked.

Minneh froze, but Amy—who'd had all morning to work out a clever response to just this question—came back with, "Sean who?"

"I don't know," Mom admitted. "Sean whoever-it-was-that-used-to-own-our-dog-before-we-did."

"Where?" Amy asked.

"Two tables down in the blue sweater."

"Everybody's sweaters are blue," Amy pointed out,

though Sean Gorman's was a distinctive electric blue. "It's the dress code."

Mom sounded exasperated. "The one that's *really* blue—that doesn't match anybody else's."

At this point Amy ran out of clever questions with which to confuse the issue.

Minneh leaned forward and said, "Amy, I bet she means Steven."

Since there wasn't a Steven in their class, Amy said, "Oh. Right. Steven."

"Steven?" Mom repeated. "Don't you think he looks like Sean?"

"No," Amy said.

"Not at all," Minneh added.

Mom looked at Minneh. "I hadn't realized you'd met Sean."

Minneh got a panicked look. She said, "I . . . didn't . . . but . . ."

Amy said, "I described him to her."

Minneh nodded her head. "And Sean's description didn't sound at all like how Steven looks."

Mr. Tannen sneezed and their candle went out yet again. Mrs. Pudlyk glared, and Mr. Tannen whispered loudly to the people at the next table, "Borrow a light?"

At least it got Mom off the subject of Sean.

Finally, after Dana's mom set the end of her scarf on fire with her table's candle, and after Jennifer's grandfather dropped the container of glitter for the second time, and after Justin's mom had to be sent to the school nurse because she had bonded her fingers together with Super Glue, Sister Mary Grace said, "Oh, my, almost time for lunch! Let's clean up, then we'll have our egg fashion show, and by then the pizzas should have arrived. Then it's good-bye till after Easter." She sounded as though she was really looking forward to the good-bye part.

So was Amy.

18

◇◆◇

THE EASTER EGG PARADE

After all the broken eggs and extinguished candle stubs and leftover bits of paper, felt, and feathers were gathered together to be thrown out, it was time for the Easter egg parade.

One by one, alphabetically, each family displayed their eggs in the clear plastic containers Mrs. Pudlyk had provided so that the eggs could be seen yet carried with minimum risk of damage.

Mrs. Pudlyk, Amy was fairly certain, would never again come to a school function. But she had a brave—if somewhat strained—smile as each family walked by.

When Sister Mary Grace got to the G's, Amy managed to scrape her chair against the floor at the same moment Minneh coughed, both on the last word of

Sister Mary Grace's announcement, "Betty Ann Gorman and her son, Sean."

"Excuse me," Minneh whispered in a delicate little voice that contrasted with the whooping-cough bellow she'd just given.

Mom clearly suspected Minneh's whole family was highly contagious, but at least she didn't seem to question the timing. Still, when the Gormans stopped in front of their table, Mom leaned closer for a better look at Sean. "Hi!" she said brightly.

" 'lo," Sean mumbled, pretending not to recognize her. In a bored but rapid monotone, he described his Ukrainian-style egg, with its stars, leaves, and windmills. He showed more enthusiasm for his second egg, which he'd decorated to look like a football.

As Mrs. Gorman moved on to the next table, Amy said, softly, "Gee, that's really neat, Steven"—with just the slightest emphasis on *Steven*, to let Sean know, just in case.

Sean caught on quickly. His voice was perfectly normal as he answered, "Thanks, Amy."

Mom was peering closely at him. "You know," she said, "we saw your twin the other day."

Perhaps Sean caught on a bit too quickly. Instead of realizing she simply meant they'd seen someone who looked remarkably like him, he assumed Amy had made up a story about his actually having a twin. "My twin," he repeated, nodding. "Yes. Sean."

"You have a twin?" Mom asked in amazement.

"Ahmmmm . . ." Sean said, confused now, stalling for time.

"I didn't know you had a twin," Amy said, to let him know he was on his own for this story.

"Yeah," Sean said. "Yeah, that's right. I'm Steven, and my brother—my twin brother—is Sean."

"So he must be in a different class," Mom said. "Since Amy didn't know him." She thought about that for a half second. "Though it's odd—"

"He goes to a different school," Sean interrupted. "My parents are divorced. So they split me and Sean up."

"How sad!" Mom gasped.

Just then Sean's mother, ready to move on from the next table, noticed how far behind he'd fallen and called, "Come on, Sean, you're holding things up."

Sean whispered to Mom, "Poor Mother. She gets confused a lot since the divorce." To make sure Mom found that reasonable, he added, "Probably because of all the drinking she does on account of trying to forget about my father running off with his aerobics instructor." He mimed drinking from a bottle.

Mom looked shocked but only said, "You poor thing."

Sean nodded and continued on to the next table.

Mr. Tannen leaned over the girls to say to Mom, "It's sad how many dysfunctional families there are these days."

She probably would have agreed more wholeheartedly if he hadn't been scratching his rash and sniffling as he said it.

When it was time for Amy and her mother to show

off their eggs, Amy insisted that Mom go first. That way, Amy, walking behind, could bump into her and keep her moving. Which was exactly what she did at the Gormans' table.

Mom ignored her. She rested her hand on Mrs. Gorman's and said, "I just wanted to tell you: If there's anything I can do—anything—you just let me know."

"Thank you," Mrs. Gorman said slowly, warily, giving Mom much the same kind of look that Mom had been giving Mr. Tannen all morning.

Wordlessly, Sean wiggled his eyebrows at Amy when he recognized the portrait of Sherlock on her egg.

Mom moved on to the next group of people at the table—the Walker-Pudlyks. Behind her back, Amy saw Sean demonstrate for his mother the same drinking-from-a-bottle bit he had done at their table about *her*.

Second to last in the parade to display their artwork were the Walker-Pudlyks. Kaitlyn's parents and grandfather hadn't even tried Ukrainian-style eggs. They'd concentrated on stickers and sequins. Kaitlyn, however, had spent the entire three hours working on one egg. And she'd worked alone, because Mrs. Pudlyk had been demonstrating for and helping other people. Kaitlyn's egg was entirely her own work.

"Kaitlyn," Amy said, amazed at the steady detail of the tiny designs, "it's gorgeous. It's like you worked on a big egg and then shrunk it down to a perfect miniature. It really *is* art."

"Thank you," Kaitlyn said, like a queen graciously accepting praise from her subjects.

Last of all came Raymond Young. Raymond's father was either dead, or on a secret mission for the CIA, or in South America with thousands of dollars of his former employer's money—depending on which rumor you believed. His mother worked two jobs and hadn't made it yet to a school function, which was why Sister Mary Grace had sat with him.

Starting with three eggs, Raymond had dropped one, then pressed too hard when penciling in his design on each of his other two. In exasperation, he'd thrown out all three, and Sister Mary Grace had donated one of her backup eggs. That now had a crack in it, too. Amy worried that Mrs. Pudlyk's plastic container was the only thing that held the egg together and that once Raymond returned it, the egg would be Humpty-Dumpty all over again.

"Eggs," Raymond said, explaining his border of lopsided circles, "because that's what this is, an egg. Ladybug, because I like ladybugs. Star at the top, because that's easy to draw."

"Very nice," Mom assured him.

As Raymond reached the last table, the one with the Gormans and the Walker-Pudlyks, there was a knock on the door and a whiff of tomato sauce and cheese. The pizza had arrived. People started to get up, to form a line before the boxes were even set down. Mom, however—Amy saw with alarm—was about to zero in on the Gormans. "Minneh," Amy whispered from between clenched teeth.

"Mrs. Prochenko," Minneh called urgently to distract her.

Mom stopped.

"Ahmmm," Minneh said. "My father and I really enjoyed meeting you, didn't we, Dad?"

Without listening for Mom's reaction, Amy ran ahead to get in a word of warning to Sean. Sean was trying to convince his mother that he had never really liked pizza, and why didn't they leave—now—and have a nice lunch at home?

Mrs. Gorman was obviously just waiting for him to stop talking so she could say, "Nonsense."

Beyond the Gormans, Sister Mary Grace was thanking Kaitlyn's family for all their help. Raymond had just managed to get his egg—mostly in one piece—out of the container so he could return the container to Kaitlyn's grandmother. Only Amy was near enough and not talking to overhear when Kaitlyn leaned close to Raymond, pinched his cheek as though she were an adult and he a chubby toddler, and said—smiling sweetly—"You're so special, Raymond. You and your egg. Don't ever let anybody tell you differently."

Raymond was not the quickest person in class and often misunderstood things. *Let him misunderstand this*, Amy wished now. *Make him think she really means it*.

But even if Kaitlyn's energetic brightness wasn't obvious enough, she added, "And I don't believe for a minute that story about your father running away from home to get away from you."

Amy's mind went blank at the viciousness of the attack. For a long moment Raymond looked at the egg in his hand. Then he closed his fist on it. He flipped his hand over, letting the pieces drop into the garbage can, brushed off the remaining sticky bits of shell, and walked back to his seat without a word.

Why? Amy thought. What possible pleasure could Kaitlyn get from saying such a hurtful thing to someone like Raymond, who could not defend himself? It was like intentionally poking a baby. Or like kicking a dog. A poor, helpless dog.

"You miserable little wretch," Amy said to Kaitlyn. She started in a whisper because that was all she could manage, but got louder with each word. "You may have made the prettiest egg, but you're a nasty, ugly person." While no one seemed to have heard Kaitlyn, everybody seemed to hear her. The room instantly fell silent, and everyone was gaping at her.

"Amy!" she heard Mom gasp.

"Amy!" Sister Mary Grace echoed, no doubt embarrassed in front of Kaitlyn's family after they had gone out of their way to be nice to her class. "Please explain what this is all about."

Raymond was watching. Did he realize she had jumped in to defend him? Would he appreciate knowing that someone had overheard him being humiliated? How could she explain without repeating in front of everyone what Kaitlyn had said and making Raymond feel even worse?

"Someday somebody's got to teach you a lesson,"

Amy told Kaitlyn. She stamped her feet all the way back to her place at her own table.

Behind her, she heard Kaitlyn say, "Oh, dear! I think she was just a little bit jealous of my egg."

Amy closed her eyes and concentrated on not crying and on not strangling Kaitlyn.

19

PICNIC

"Amy."

Amy felt Minneh lean over her, but she kept her eyes closed.

"Sherlock is fine," Minneh whispered, obviously thinking that Amy was just overly worried about him. "And I asked my mother if I could have a friend spend the night tonight, and she said yes, if it's OK with your mother, and then you'll see."

Amy felt Minneh straighten, then Mom's voice said, "Amy, what was that all about?" Then, more sharply, "Amy."

Amy opened her eyes and saw Mom and Sister Mary Grace. Mr. Tannen was motioning Minneh to leave them alone together. Other people were working very hard at ignoring them. "It isn't fair," Amy said. "Everyone thinks Kaitlyn is so wonderful, but she isn't." Mom started to protest, but Amy continued without giving her a chance. "She says mean things and nobody ever notices."

"She told you your egg was very nice," Mom pointed out.

"She didn't mean it," Amy protested, which wasn't the point, but she didn't know what else to say.

"I can't believe you'd embarrass me like this," Mom said. "Why are you behaving this way?"

Sister Mary Grace put a hand on Mom's arm. "Normally Amy behaves very well," she said. "Sometimes, too many things happen at once and overwhelm us." She looked sympathetically at Amy.

It's not fair, Amy thought. None of it was fair. Kaitlyn. Dr. Boden. Life. *It's not fair.*

"And it's not fair"—Amy jumped, hearing Sister Mary Grace speak out loud the words she'd just been saying in her mind, then Sister Mary Grace finished—"to say, 'Everyone this . . .' and 'Nobody that . . .' Sometimes people notice things you don't think they do. But still: You cannot lash out at people. Do you understand?"

"I think so," Amy said, though uncertainly. Then, even more uncertainly, she thought, *Sister Mary Grace* doesn't *think Kaitlyn is wonderful?*

Sister Mary Grace told Mom, "I think we can forgive one uncharacteristic outburst, don't you?"

Mom nodded, but slowly.

Amy wondered if that would last only as long as Sister Mary Grace was there. She had the feeling she was about to find out, just as one of the parents exclaimed, "Yes, a picnic!"

Immediately two or three others agreed that a picnic was a fine idea.

"Oh," Sister Mary Grace called over as people started to pick up the food to bring outdoors, "that's so much work, to get the tables and chairs out . . ."

Someone's mother said, "We just need one of the small tables, to hold the pizza and the drinks. There's plenty of room for sitting in the playground. And look—here's Bill, fresh and strong and just in time to carry the table."

The man who'd just entered said, "I had a morning meeting that I thought would never end. Have I missed everything?"

"No, you're just in time to move this table," the pushy mother said.

"Who's that?" Mom asked Amy as Sister Mary Grace rushed away from them to help clear the table.

"Sean's father," Amy said, recognizing him from field trips. She suddenly realized what she'd said. She added, hoping she sounded nonchalant, "I guess. Because he's Steven's father, too."

"Hmpf!" Mom said.

All the pizza boxes and jugs of fruit juice had already been taken. Mr. Gorman began folding the small table's legs.

"Come, Amy," Mom said, heading for the door.

Amy took a deep breath and hoped for the best.

Mr. Gorman smiled at them as they whisked by.

"Beast," Mom snarled at him.

Amy didn't dare hesitate to see his reaction. The most she could do now was to stick close to her mother to try to keep her from offering any more sympathy to Mrs. Gorman.

But as soon as they stepped outside, Sean and Minneh came running up calling, "Amy! Amy!"

And following them—for a moment she was thrilled, but then her heart sank—was Sherlock. What was he doing here? He was supposed to be safely away, hiding in Minneh's garage. Had Dr. Boden tracked him there? Had he tracked him *here*?

She looked up and down the street but saw no sign of him or his car.

"Oh, look!" Mom said. "Steven and Minneh found your dog."

Kaitlyn came running up, too. But she, obviously, wasn't looking for Amy. "Sister Mary Grace! Sister Mary Grace!"

"Yes, Kaitlyn?" Sister Mary Grace said.

"Look." Kaitlyn pointed. "Amy's dog is here. You said he wasn't allowed to come back, and Amy brought him anyway."

"Kaitlyn, dear," Sister Mary Grace said, "you really must learn to mind your own business and to stop tattling."

Amy felt as though she'd waited all her life to hear this. But much as she longed to hear more, she had to get to Sherlock.

Sherlock knew enough to run to the far end of the playground, leading Amy, Sean, and Minneh away from the cluster of picnicking adults. When he stopped, Amy threw herself to her knees and flung her arms around his neck. "Oh, Sherlock!" she said. "I've missed you, and I'm glad to see you, but you shouldn't have come. How will I ever explain to Mom that we can't bring you home? And we can't: Dr. Boden was there last night."

Sherlock scratched with his back leg, making his collar jingle, and looked at Minneh.

There wasn't time for complicated secrecy. "Oh," Amy said in exasperation, "it's all right. Minneh's got to learn eventually. Minneh, Sherlock can talk."

"Speak, Sherlock," Minneh said, obviously expecting a bark.

Sherlock said, "I had to leave the garage when Minneh and her father came in to get the truck to drive to school this morning."

Minneh's mouth dropped open.

Sherlock continued, "The people from the college must have seen that I wasn't at your house anymore, and they must have been looking around the neighborhood, because all of a sudden I noticed that Dr. Schieber was following me."

All three children looked up, even Minneh, who hadn't yet gotten around to closing her mouth. Across the street was a well-dressed woman who looked older than Mom but younger than Sister Mary Grace. "That woman?" Amy asked. "She's a doctor, too? Like Dr. Boden?"

"Actually," Sherlock said, "Dr. Schieber is the head of the department—she's Dr. Boden's boss."

"Oh boy," Sean muttered.

Sherlock said, "Amy, this isn't working. I'm only getting you deeper and deeper in trouble. But I couldn't leave without saying good-bye."

"Good-bye?" Amy squealed. "Where are you going?"

"I don't know," Sherlock admitted. "But I'm going to start running, and I'm going to try to find places Dr. Schieber can't follow with her car. I won't be able to come back, Amy, because they'll be watching you."

"But how will you get along?" Amy cried. "You've never been out in the world; there's all sorts of things you don't know, smart as you are. Who'll feed you? Where will you go to stay out of the weather?"

But she knew he was right.

She only wasted time by denying it.

She took a shaky breath. Later. Later she could worry about her broken heart. She said, "You know to stay away from Animal Control, and you must be careful of streets, too; lots of dogs get hit by cars—"

"Yikes," Minneh interrupted, finally getting her mouth to do something more than hang open, "the doc's headed this way."

"Go to kids," Amy told Sherlock, frantic to fit in last-second instructions, to delay—even for a few moments—what was coming. "Don't trust grown-ups; trust kids. They can't help you as much, but they're less likely to turn you in."

"Good-bye, Amy," Sherlock said. "Thank you."

"Wait until she's almost here," Sean advised Sherlock. "Then take off across the church parking lot to that hole in the fence. She'll have to go all the way back to her car."

"In fact," Amy said, realizing how lucky Sherlock had been—since he might have sought help from someone like Kaitlyn—"next time, don't ask for help. Don't talk until you get to know the person."

"Closing in," Minneh warned.

"I'll never forget you," Sherlock said.

Amy could feel his muscles tense up, ready, waiting just another moment to flee, and her words ran out.

"There!" a voice cried. "There she is!" But it wasn't the department head from the college. It was Kaitlyn, coming up behind them. She was pointing a finger at Amy. "Thief!" she cried. "Sister Mary Grace won't be able to ignore this. You're in real trouble now, Amy Prochenko! *I've* called the police!"

20

◆◇◆

DR. SCHIEBER

Run!" Amy told Sherlock.

But he hesitated, watching Kaitlyn's approach. And Dr. Schieber was close enough to call without shouting: "F-32."

"Go!" Amy tried to shove Sherlock away.

"You're in trouble," Sherlock said.

"We knew that already." She smacked his rump with her hand.

"But it can't be because of me," Sherlock pointed out. "Kaitlyn doesn't know I belong to the college. She couldn't have called the police about you stealing *me*."

"Kaitlyn doesn't matter. *Run*, Sherlock."

But it was already too late.

Dr. Schieber put out her hand toward Sherlock. "F-32," she said.

Sherlock growled, baring his teeth.

Dr. Schieber rested her hand on his head as though it never occurred to her that he might really bite. "Stop it," she said in a gentle but no-nonsense voice.

Sherlock stopped it.

By then Kaitlyn had reached them, with Mom and Sister Mary Grace only a few steps behind, and the rest of the class and their families approaching fast.

Kaitlyn was breathing hard from running across the yard while simultaneously shouting. "You are in *so* much trouble, Amy," she said now. "I can't believe what a sneaky no-good lowlife you are. The police are going to arrest you and put you in jail, and you'll have a prison record for the rest of your worthless life, and you'll end up living on the street, a homeless bum."

Sherlock growled at Kaitlyn, much more fiercely than he had done for Dr. Schieber.

Dr. Schieber held her hand up to warn Sherlock to stop, but she addressed Kaitlyn. Amazingly, she asked, "Is all this hysterical name-calling absolutely necessary?"

Kaitlyn was momentarily left speechless, and by then Mom and Sister Mary Grace arrived, demanding to know what had happened.

"Amy stole my egg," Kaitlyn said.

"What?" Amy asked. Eggs had been the last thing on her mind.

The rest of the crowd started to arrive and began

asking questions, and Kaitlyn got her wind back. "You all heard her," Kaitlyn shouted. "She was jealous of me, so she stole my egg. She threatened to teach me a lesson."

"Young lady, stop screeching," Sister Mary Grace said.

"Thank you," Dr. Schieber told Sister Mary Grace. She gingerly touched her temple as though Kaitlyn had been giving her a headache. She ignored Sister Mary Grace's puzzled "And who are you?" look and asked, "All this is about an egg?"

Kaitlyn took several deep breaths. She must have realized that shouting was getting her nowhere, so she switched from furious to hurt-but-brave. "I'm sorry I was yelling," she said to Sister Mary Grace. "It's just I was so upset that Amy could do such a hateful thing. I know it's not normally like her." She turned back to Dr. Schieber. "What she stole was a Ukrainian Easter egg," she said. "I spent all morning making it, and Amy was jealous because hers wasn't nearly as good as mine."

"That's not true," Amy said.

"Mine *was* better," Kaitlyn insisted, calmly but firmly. "Ask anyone."

Amy said, "I mean, *yes*, mine wasn't as good as yours, but *no*, I wasn't jealous. And *definitely no*, I didn't take it."

Dr. Schieber cut off Kaitlyn's protest. "And you called the police because your egg is missing?" she asked in that never-get-excited voice of hers. "And they agreed to come? For an egg?"

Kaitlyn pouted a bit that Dr. Schieber refused to get upset. "It was a Ukrainian egg," she explained again. "I dialed 911. I said there'd been a theft at the school."

"Ah," Dr. Schieber said.

Amy had just been thinking that if she hadn't known about Sherlock and the experiment, she would have thought the calm and soft-spoken Dr. Schieber was nice. But now Dr. Schieber smiled at Kaitlyn, a smile that made Amy think, *I bet this is how a snake smiles, right before it opens its mouth and swallows up a mouse, whole.* She was glad that—for the moment, for whatever reason—the mouse seemed to be Kaitlyn.

Beside Amy, Sherlock stood perfectly still, watching.

Dr. Schieber said, "So you knew not to tell the police exactly why they were being summoned: 'Help, help, I've been robbed,' then *click!* you hang up before they can ask for details?"

Kaitlyn squirmed.

Mr. Walker stepped forward. "Why are you cross-examining my daughter?" he asked Dr. Schieber. "*She's* the victim here."

Kaitlyn snuggled up to him, her bottom lip trembling as though she were fighting back tears, and she nodded to emphasize what her father had just said.

Dr. Schieber never looked at Mr. Walker. She told Kaitlyn, "For a victim, you sound as though you have a guilty conscience."

"She stole my Ukrainian Easter egg," Kaitlyn whimpered. "Everyone heard her threaten to, then she went ahead and did it."

Dr. Schieber looked at Amy.

"It's not true," Amy said, trying to sound as calm as Dr. Schieber.

"People *heard*," Kaitlyn repeated.

"I *said*," Amy explained, "that somebody needed to teach her a lesson. I wasn't talking about her Easter egg, and she knows it."

"Her egg wasn't as nice as mine," Kaitlyn insisted, refusing to get off that topic. Mournfully, generously, she added, "If I could share my talent, I would."

"I think," Dr. Schieber said, "perhaps we should investigate the crime scene, before the police arrive and embarrass us."

"*I* think," Mr. Walker said, "you need to tell us who you are, and why you're in this school yard."

Kaitlyn nodded in solemn agreement.

"My name is Dr. Karen Schieber, and I'm the owner of this dog. He's been lost for several days, and I just located him."

Before the Walkers could say anything, Mom said, "*You* own this dog?" Then, her eyes grew wider. "*You're* the aerobics instructor"—even she didn't sound as though she believed it, probably because Dr. Schieber looked old enough to be a grandmother— "who ran off with"—she pointed at Sean—"this boy's father?"

Sean's mother said, *"What?"*

Sean's father said, "I—I—I—I—"

"Aerobics instructor?" Dr. Schieber sounded more concerned about being mistaken for an aerobics instructor than about being mistaken for someone who ran off with people's fathers. "No, I'm head of the Biological Research Department at the college. However"—she turned back to Mr. Walker—"that's neither here nor there." She gave another of those cold-blooded smiles. "This situation needs to be investigated. Come." She beckoned to follow, and Amy wasn't sure if she meant Amy herself, or Sherlock, or Mr. Walker, or the whole crowd. "Let's see if we can't find this egg."

Sherlock followed right on her heels, never even glancing back at Amy. *Come back,* she wanted to tell him. *Now's your chance, while nobody's paying attention to you.* But there was no way to get to him. Half the crowd was between them, following Dr. Schieber back into the school. *No wonder she's the head of the department,* Amy thought. Whatever else, when she gave instructions, people obeyed.

Behind her, Amy heard Mr. Gorman telling his wife, "But, dear, I don't even take aerobics . . ."

Mom rested her hand on Amy's shoulder as they walked. "You didn't take it?" Mom's voice was somewhere between saying and asking. "Not even temporarily, intending to give it back, just to teach her a lesson?"

"No," Amy said.

Mom smiled. "I knew that," she said. "I had to ask."

Amy nodded.

Mom said, "The dog's owner?"

Once again, Amy nodded.

"I'm so confused."

Amy tried not to sigh, since her mother's confusion was all Amy's fault. She said, "I'll explain later."

21

◇ ◆ ◇

THE SCENE OF THE CRIME

*D*r. Schieber said to Sister Mary Grace, "You don't mind my bringing my dog into the school building with me, do you? He's very well behaved."

Sister Mary Grace looked from Dr. Schieber to Sherlock to Amy, and obviously decided now was not the time to try to sort out that particular situation. She gestured to go ahead.

"Now," Dr. Schieber asked, "where did this theft take place?"

"From here," Kaitlyn answered, indicating the cafeteria. She gave a weak sniffle, then shouldered her way to the front of the crowd to lead them.

"My grandmother and I," Kaitlyn said self-importantly, "gave a demonstration on how to make

Ukrainian Easter eggs. My family left our things here." She showed where she had been sitting. "My egg was in this cup." Being the instructor's granddaughter, she had better supplies than the plastic containers the others had used. "I came back inside to get our stuff together," Kaitlyn said, "because we were getting ready to go. That's when I saw that *she* had taken it."

"That's when you saw that it was missing," Sister Mary Grace corrected. "Could you have put it someplace else, Kaitlyn, and forgotten?" She poked at Mrs. Pudlyk's big wicker basket full of supplies.

"No," Kaitlyn said, in a "Boy, is that a stupid thought" tone that would have gotten anybody else under any other circumstances into trouble. She pulled out the photo album and turned to the last page. She told Dr. Schieber, "I made all of these last year. The one I made today looked something like this one, except even better."

"And where was Amy sitting?" Dr. Schieber asked.

Kaitlyn pointed.

Dr. Schieber and the whole crowd shifted down several tables. In the Easter grass–lined box Mom had brought from home were the eggs Amy and Mom had made. Dr. Schieber reached out but didn't touch Amy's egg with the dog and flowers. "F-32," she said, recognizing the picture despite the fact that even Amy knew it wasn't a very good one. She smiled—a regular smile as opposed to her snake smile.

"What?" someone from the crowd asked. "What did she say?"

Dr. Schieber turned her cold look onto Kaitlyn. "I don't see your egg."

She's helping me, Amy thought in astonishment. But then she wondered: *Why?*

Kaitlyn tossed her hair. "Well, even Amy wouldn't be stupid enough to put it right there where anybody could see."

"Kaitlyn," Sister Mary Grace warned.

"Sorry, Sister Mary Grace," Kaitlyn said.

Dr. Schieber said, "Do you think she put it in her locker? Hid it, perhaps, to take out later?"

Kaitlyn shrugged. "I don't know."

Again that smile that would have sent shivers down Amy's spine if it had been directed toward her. "Well then," Dr. Schieber suggested as though from a great distance away, "perhaps we should go look?"

Amy led the way to her locker. She was so nervous about everybody looking on—with some of them, she was sure, convinced she was a thief—that it took her two tries before she got the combination right.

Sister Mary Grace took the extra sweater Amy had hanging from the hook and pulled the pockets inside out. Nothing more than tissues, mostly unused; a pencil stub with no point; and an empty gum wrapper. At least she didn't lecture Amy about the gum wrapper in school. Next she picked up Amy's gym clothes that were in a heap at the bottom of the locker, and tipped the sneakers to show that there were no eggs hidden in the toes. She took down the wobbly pile of notebooks and papers from the shelf, and even looked through the used lunch bags that had accumulated from those days Amy brought a sandwich because she hadn't liked whatever the cafeteria was serving. Most of the bags just held a used napkin and the wax paper the sandwich had been wrapped in, but one held an orange, turned fuzzy and green.

"Nothing," Sister Mary Grace said, keeping the lunch bags to throw away herself.

"How odd," Dr. Schieber said, not sounding as though she really found it odd at all. What was she up to? She asked, "Where else could that pesky egg be?"

"Maybe she didn't want to keep it," Kaitlyn said. "Maybe she just didn't want me to have it."

"She could have thrown it away," Dr. Schieber said. She gave a long look at the armload of lunch bags Sister Mary Grace was holding. "Well, you know, she doesn't really strike me as one who likes to throw away much, but I suppose it's worth a look." She headed back to the cafeteria. "Come, F-32," she called, because Sherlock was hanging back.

He'd probably just realized that now would be a good time to make a break for it, Amy thought. She leaned down to give him a hug. "I'll be fine," she whispered. But now Dr. Schieber was watching. Amy told him, "Next time she turns her back, run."

Sherlock barked, though it'd take a lot more than not talking to convince Dr. Schieber that he wasn't who she knew he was.

Amy and Sherlock and the crowd followed Dr. Schieber back into the cafeteria. There were several big garbage cans, and Dr. Schieber peered into the one closest to the door.

"See!" Kaitlyn said. "All sorts of broken eggs in here."

"That's because everybody was throwing their mistakes away," Minneh's father said, interrupting the blowing of his nose to say it. "There's one of mine in there that I dropped when I sneezed, and one of Minneh's she didn't like."

Mom's grateful look said, Amy was sure, that she forgave him all his sneezing and snuffling and scratching, since he'd defended her daughter.

"This could be it." Kaitlyn pointed. "See how it's all smushed—not just cracked, but even the inside part is all broken up like she tried to pulverize it so nobody would recognize it."

Amy looked. "That's Raymond's egg," she said.

"Where *is* Raymond?" Sister Mary Grace asked.

"He went home," said Adam, who got along with everyone and was one of Raymond's few friends. "He didn't stay for lunch."

"That's convenient," Kaitlyn said. "Amy probably saw him leave. She likes him, you know," she added in a belittling singsong, "so she would have been watching. So she knew she could say this one was his and he wouldn't be here to say yes or no."

Amy, who felt sorry for Raymond but had never counted him as a friend, much less a boyfriend, said nothing.

"Anyway," Kaitlyn said, "even if that one turns out to be Raymond's, Amy might just have buried mine in deeper under all the garbage. Or she may have put it in another garbage can. Or she might have thrown it outside. Or she might have fed it to her dog." Kaitlyn suddenly caught up to things. "Excuse me, I mean the dog she lied and said was hers that really belongs to this lady."

Sherlock barked at her.

"If he bites," Kaitlyn's mother warned, "believe me, we'll sue."

"He doesn't bite," Dr. Schieber said.

Sherlock stood on his hind legs and leaned against the garbage can, sniffing at the contents.

"Does he knock over garbage cans?" Kaitlyn asked.

At which point a uniformed policeman walked into the room. "Someone call 911 to report a robbery?" he asked.

22

◇◆◇

INVESTIGATING

Kaitlyn pointed at Amy. She told the policeman, "I'm sorry to say that this girl, a known liar, has stolen valuable property, including this lady's dog and my Ukrainian Easter egg."

"This girl," Dr. Schieber countered before the policeman could say anything, "took good care of my dog after he strayed, and I'm very grateful to her."

Kaitlyn said, "Everybody heard her say it was her dog."

"And he was," Dr. Schieber said, "since she was the one taking care of him for those days."

"That wasn't what she said," Kaitlyn muttered.

Dr. Schieber smiled brightly. "I certainly didn't call 911"—she glanced at the policeman's name tag—"Officer Munshi."

The policeman looked at Kaitlyn. "And what's this about a . . . an *egg*, did you say?"

"A Ukrainian Easter egg," Kaitlyn explained. She tried to show him the photo album, but he wasn't interested.

"You called 9ll for a missing egg?"

"These eggs can be quite valuable," Mrs. Pudlyk said in defense of her granddaughter and of the tradition of Ukrainian Easter eggs. "Some have sold at the auctions for two or three thousand dollars."

Officer Munshi took out a pad of paper and poised a pen over it. "This egg was worth between two and three thousand dollars?"

"Well"—Mrs. Pudlyk glanced away—"not this particular egg."

Officer Munshi clicked his pen twice: point in, point out. "How much," he asked, sounding just the slightest bit impatient, "do you estimate this particular egg was worth?"

Mom said, "At eighty-nine cents a dozen on special this week at Wegmans, that would be approximately seven and a half cents."

Officer Munshi clicked his pen several times as people in the crowd snickered. Except, of course, for the Walker-Pudlyks.

"Not counting, of course," Mom admitted, "the time and expense of hard-boiling it."

"It was worth more than that!" Kaitlyn stamped her foot.

Officer Munshi put his pad away.

"I worked all morning on it," Kaitlyn cried, getting

loud once again, "and Amy stole it because she was jealous. Look!" She grabbed up Amy's egg from its box. "See how ugly hers is? See why she was jealous?"

"Kaitlyn," Sister Mary Grace started, "be—" But before she could say "careful," the egg dropped from Kaitlyn's hand.

Amy saw it falling, falling, falling, and was unable to move. Then it smashed on the floor.

Sherlock barked sharply.

"Oh!" Kaitlyn said. Even Amy couldn't be 100 percent sure she had done it on purpose. In the total stillness of the crowded room, Kaitlyn said, "I'm so sorry. I didn't mean to drop it. I was just trying to show why she was so jealous."

Sean stooped to pick up the egg—which was good, because Amy still couldn't move at all. One side of the egg was crushed, mostly where the flowers were; but crack lines webbed out over most of the lopsided picture of Sherlock. Sean gently set the egg back down in the Easter grass. A piece of shell stuck to his finger.

"I didn't mean it," Kaitlyn repeated sulkily.

Sherlock barked again.

Officer Munshi looked from Kaitlyn to Amy to Sister Mary Grace. "Who called 911?" Amy could tell he was getting angry. He was still glaring at Sister Mary Grace despite the fact that she was shaking her head. "Don't you realize that while I'm here listening to these children bicker, something serious could be happening somewhere else in the city? First you tie up 911's phone line, then you take me off the streets to listen to this squabbling because you don't have control of your class—"

"I beg your pardon!" Sister Mary Grace objected. "Kaitlyn Walker took it upon herself to call you. I had nothing to do with it, and neither did any of the other adults."

"No control," Officer Munshi repeated.

Sherlock stood right in front of him and once more barked.

"And as for this dog," Officer Munshi said, "don't you know there's a public health ordinance against dogs inside school buildings, except for Seeing Eye dogs?"

Sherlock barked again.

"It almost looks," Dr. Schieber said innocently, "as though he's trying to tell you something, doesn't it?"

Amy felt chilled, not knowing what Dr. Schieber planned.

Sherlock bobbed his head and barked again.

"You're lucky," Officer Munshi said, "I don't write the whole lot of you up for calling in a frivolous report, and for . . ." He paused, trying to think of something, and Dr. Schieber suggested, "Obstructing justice?"

By his look, he was seriously considering it, at least for her. Instead, he turned and started out of the room.

Sherlock kept moving in front of him, barking all the time.

"Lady, curb this dog of yours."

"I really think he wants to tell you something," Dr. Schieber said.

Is she trying to force Sherlock into actually speaking? Amy wondered. Not likely, if the experiment at the college was supposed to be secret. She wouldn't want Officer Munshi and all the kids and parents here to know. But Amy could tell Sherlock was getting frustrated, not being able to communicate with the policeman in normal-dog fashion. He stood in the way, looking directly into Officer Munshi's eyes, backing up only to keep from getting stepped on.

"Sherlock," Amy said, "why don't you show me, and I'll show Officer Munshi?"

Sherlock barked once in agreement, then whirled and ran down the hall, the opposite direction Officer Munshi had been trying to go, back toward Amy's locker.

Amy glanced over her shoulder and saw that the policeman was at least giving her a minute. He lingered in the hallway as though ready to run if he even suspected he was being made fun of.

"What is it, Sherlock?" Amy said.

Sherlock barked rather than spoke because several of the children and parents were close on Amy's heels.

At Amy's locker, Sherlock stopped, then started back the way he'd just come, toward the cafeteria and—beyond that—Officer Munshi, and—beyond him—the door.

"This is ridiculous!" Officer Munshi said in exasperation, and once more faced the door.

"No, look," said Mr. Tannen, Minneh's father. "He's sniffing."

Something Mom probably figured Mr. Tannen knew all about. But he was right: Sherlock was sniffing at the lockers. And suddenly he stopped in front of one of them. He gave a sharp bark.

Nobody moved.

Sherlock sat down and gave a long, loud wolf howl.

"Jeez!" Officer Munshi winced at the noise. But he came closer. "What is it?" he asked Amy. "What's he saying?" Amy started to shake her head, and he asked, "Whose locker is this?"

"I'm not sure," Amy said. "But these are all fifth graders' lockers."

Officer Munshi turned to include everyone in his question. "Whose locker is this?" he repeated. "Number 210?" When nobody answered, he said, "Surely there are records in the office."

"I'll check," Sister Mary Grace offered.

"Mine." It was Kaitlyn who stepped forward. "The stupid dog has pointed out *my* locker. Stupid dog."

"Please open it, Miss," Officer Munshi said.

"Daddy," Kaitlyn said, "doesn't he need a search warrant or something?"

Her father hesitated then said, "Open the locker, Kaits."

Scowling, Kaitlyn unfastened the lock.

Not that it meant anything, but Amy was relieved to see that it looked no neater than her own.

Officer Munshi reached to the shelf and pulled out a knitted cap. Nestled inside was Kaitlyn's egg.

"I hate you," Kaitlyn told Amy, "and the way everybody always makes such a fuss about you and your stupid dog that isn't even your own dog."

"Me?" Amy squeaked. Wasn't it enough for Kaitlyn to be the most-liked girl in fifth grade? She had to be the *only* liked one?

Officer Munshi crooked his finger at the Walker-Pudlyks. He asked Sister Mary Grace, "Is there a room where I can speak privately with you and the family?"

"Certainly," Sister Mary Grace said solemnly. "Follow me."

23

❖◇❖

SOME OF THE TRUTH

*P*eople began to drift back to the cafeteria to pick up their things and leave.

Amy tried to silently catch Sherlock's attention, making frantic hand signals for him to head out the door.

Sean sidled up to her. "You sure bring excitement into the school year," he said, which was certainly not something anyone had ever told Amy before. "Do you think they'll arrest her for making a false police report?"

Behind him, Dr. Schieber said, "Sorry to disappoint you, young man, but she'll probably just get a good long lecture."

Sean jumped, and the excited smile on his face disappeared as he looked from Amy to Dr. Schieber to Sherlock—Sherlock, who was still there despite Amy's efforts.

"I think," Dr. Schieber said, "that some of us need to have our own private talk."

Mr. Tannen, who'd stayed because Minneh had, now said, between sniffles, "Come on, Minneh."

"Actually," Dr. Schieber said, "from what I saw outside, I believe your daughter is one of the people I need to talk with."

Mr. Tannen looked suspiciously at Minneh and asked Dr. Schieber, "Is she in some sort of trouble?"

Dr. Schieber laughed, and it was—Amy was surprised—a pleasant laugh. "Not at all."

Whatever Minneh felt, at least Amy was relieved.

"Then," Mr. Tannen said, "I think *I* better leave. Dr. Schieber, that is one remarkable dog you've got—smart, and a good sniffer." He tapped the side of his nose. Sherlock gave a thank-you bark. "But I'm incredibly allergic to animals, as you've probably noticed, and something in this school got me going even before he came in. I'm going to go home and take some allergy medicine. Will you be OK, Minneh?"

Minneh nodded, looking worried and guilty.

Mom said, "We'll drive her home in a bit."

"Thank you," Mr. Tannen said, his voice stuffy from congestion. "You're a very kind lady."

Now Mom looked worried and guilty, no doubt for all her bad thoughts regarding him.

Mr. Tannen nodded good-bye and started for the door.

"Ahm, Dad," Minneh said.

He stopped and waited for her to go on.

"You might just want to"—she shrugged—"you know, vacuum out the front seat of the truck. And kind of . . . put your sweater in the wash."

Mr. Tannen thought that over. "I may just do that," he said in his slow way. He nodded once more and left.

Sean's parents were the only ones remaining, Sean having refused to take their hints and—in fact—their little shoves to get him moving away. Mrs. Gorman looked offended by Mr. Tannen's having called Mom nice. She said, "Well, I'm glad that Amy, here, was proven innocent, since Sean tells us that she's a good friend of his, and because that Kaitlyn Walker has always struck me as an insincere little sneak. But you, Mrs. Prochenko, are one strange cookie, trying to cause trouble between me and my husband."

Mom obviously didn't know what to say.

And it wasn't up to her, anyway. Gently, Amy said, "No, she's not. I'm sorry, Mrs. Gorman, it's all my fault. Kaitlyn was right about one thing: I *am* a liar. I told my mother stories, and she believed me. It's not her fault at all."

Amy didn't know what to make of the look Mom was giving her.

"And it isn't all Amy's fault, either," Sean admitted. "I told a lot of lies, too."

"All right, all right," Minneh said, cracking under the pressure although her father wasn't even there to hear her confession. "So did I."

Dr. Schieber broke the uneasy silence. "Why don't we all go sit in one of the classrooms?" she suggested.

Amy led the way to Sister Mary Grace's room. The children sat in their usual seats, and the parents squeezed themselves into desks around them. Sherlock lay down by Amy's feet.

Dr. Schieber sat on the edge of Sister Mary Grace's desk. "As I said," she started, "I'm Dr. Karen Schieber, and I'm head of the Biological Research Department at the State College of New York at Rochester. One of our projects is an attempt to increase intelligence by a combination of gene-splicing and neuron stimulation."

"Huh?" Minneh said.

Which was exactly what Amy had been thinking.

Even the grown-ups looked relieved that someone had asked.

"Basically," Dr. Schieber explained, "we're trying to increase the size of people's brains, and then cause those brains to work more efficiently."

Sean's father nodded as though to say he'd known all along.

"Naturally," Dr. Schieber said, "we couldn't just jump in and start experimenting on humans."

Everybody turned and looked at Sherlock, who yawned, then began licking his foreleg as though he'd just decided it needed a cleaning.

"Hence, F-32, whom some of you call Sherlock."

"Or Big Red," Mom said.

Dr. Schieber looked skeptical but said, "If you so desire."

Mrs. Gorman looked skeptical, too, and moved her chair the tiniest bit farther away from Mom's. Obviously Amy's confession wasn't enough to convince her of Mom's normalcy.

"So," Mr. Gorman said, "exactly how smart *is* this dog of yours?"

"Smart enough to try pretending I've got the wrong dog here," Dr. Schieber said.

Sherlock never missed a lick.

"Though he should remember I've known him so long I listened to his heartbeat with a stethoscope before he was born." She leaned forward and said, "F-32, I know it's you, and I can prove it's you because we've got your DNA records back at the lab."

Sherlock stopped licking.

"So." Dr. Schieber sat back again. "He's smart enough to reason, to listen to reason—and to talk."

Mrs. Gorman looked out the window, no doubt convinced Mom's weirdness was contagious, and that Dr. Schieber had caught it.

"F-32, please speak."

Don't! Amy thought, but Sherlock stood up. With his tail drooping in resignation, he said, "I'd like to thank you, Mrs. Prochenko, and Mr. and Mrs. Gorman, for raising kind and generous children who tried their best to help me. Any stories they made up were because they wanted to protect me."

24

All of the Truth

O h, my goodness."

Amy wasn't sure which of the women said it—Mom or Mrs. Gorman. Both were fanning themselves.

Dr. Schieber said, "F-32—" But then she leaned forward again. "Or do you prefer Sherlock?" she asked. "Or"—she hesitated but then said it anyway—"Big Red?"

"Sherlock," Sherlock said.

Dr. Schieber nodded. "Sherlock," she told them, "was doing very well—as you can see. Then suddenly, Monday morning he was gone. We were all terribly worried: What had happened to him? Had he been kidnapped by animal-rights activists worried that we might be mistreating him? Or taken by a researcher at a rival institution? He pretty much had the run of our lab. Could he have somehow injured himself during the night, gotten confused, and wandered off? We looked all around the neighborhood, made inquiries. Then, that evening, one of our graduate students spotted him, Mrs. Prochenko, in your yard, playing with your daughter."

Mom clasped Amy's hand.

"Rachel was almost certain it was him, but he wouldn't come to her, wouldn't acknowledge her. He was obviously fine and being taken care of, but he chose not to come. Strange. Rachel couldn't understand why, and neither could I when Rachel told me. So the next day, I sent another of the students to watch to see if he could learn what was going on. *After I went to the police station to vouch for him*"— Dr. Schieber leaned forward and narrowed her eyes a bit but didn't seem genuinely upset, though Minneh sank low into her seat—"I could only come to one conclusion: Our dog had simply run away. Obviously he had opportunity to return if he wanted. Why didn't he want to? So, this morning I had a long conversation with Dr. Boden, who was heading the project. 'Could something here have made F-32 so unhappy,' I asked him, 'that he doesn't want to return?' Dr. Boden assured me he had no idea what that something could be."

Amy and Sherlock both started to fidget. Sean sat up straighter as though he was about to say something.

"But I'm persistent," Dr. Schieber said. "And

finally he told me. He told me that Sherlock might have overheard him talking about dissecting Sherlock's brain."

"*What?*" Mom said.

The Gormans looked at each other in horror.

"No!" Minneh gasped.

Dr. Schieber waved an arm to indicate all of them. "My reaction exactly," she said. "Here we have this delightful test subject. And as if it's not wonderful enough how smart he is, he's bighearted, and gentle, and eager to learn, and even more eager to please, and he's funny—I mean that in the nicest way—and just generally an agreeable part of our department who fits in even better than some of the students." She considered. "*Much* better than the members of the hockey team."

"Thank you," Sherlock said, shy and surprised.

"So I said to myself"—Dr. Schieber held out both her hands as though weighing two separate things— "F-32 or Dr. Boden? Sweet, smart, easy to get along with—or someone who'd dissect a colleague's brain?" She put her hands down and smiled. "So I fired Dr. Boden."

"Good for you!" Mom said.

"Yay!" Sean and Minneh cheered.

Amy was too relieved to say anything.

Dr. Schieber continued, "Of course, Dr. Boden protested that F-32—Pardon me that I keep calling you that, Sherlock, but that's how we referred to you in our conversations . . ."

Sherlock nodded to indicate he understood.

"Dr. Boden protested that F-32 had learned everything there was to learn in the lab. I disagree, except . . ." Again she smiled.

She did have a nice smile, Amy decided, when she wasn't zeroing in on you.

"Except," Dr. Schieber repeated, "I think at this point you could learn more *outside* the lab. If only"— she looked up at the ceiling innocently—"we could find a nice, trustworthy, respectable family to take you in."

Amy's hand shot up into the air to volunteer. Belatedly she glanced at her mother for permission, which came in a nod. Amy waved her arm.

"All right, Sherlock?" Dr. Schieber asked, even though Sherlock was wagging his tail so hard it was thumping against the side of Amy's desk.

"Yes, yes, yes," Sherlock said.

"Of course, the college will provide for food and medical expenses and reading material and an Internet account and a voice-recognition computer for him so that he doesn't gum up your computer by pressing the keys with a pencil eraser."

"Oops." Sherlock slunk down guiltily.

"In return, we would like you to bring him to the lab once a month—say the first Saturday of each month—so we can check his progress, see if we need to increase his required reading—he's a terrible speller, you know. That sort of thing."

Amy and Sherlock and Mom, and even Minneh and the Gormans, all nodded eagerly.

"Then it's settled." Dr. Schieber stood and went

to shake everybody's hand or paw. "Understand, we want him to have as normal a life as possible. For the moment, while he's one of a kind, that means not letting other people in on quite how smart he is, or all the talk shows would be after him continually for interviews. But other than that, expose him to all you can think of. The more new experiences, the better. Let him watch TV, go on vacation with you, read comic books if he wants, meet other animals. Cats, even."

Sherlock shuddered, and Dr. Schieber laughed to show that she was just teasing about the cats.

"Yeah," Sean said, "you can finally meet Big Red, whose collar you've been wearing. Mom, do you have that picture in your wallet still?"

While Mrs. Gorman searched through her purse, Dr. Schieber stopped in front of Amy and said, though not unkindly, "You know, I think we could have saved a lot of trouble if you had been up front with your parents to begin with."

Amy hung her head but nodded.

Dr. Schieber nudged her chin up. "Next time," she said.

Amy nodded some more.

"I knew you hadn't stolen that awful girl's egg. I'd been watching Sherlock since before everybody came out of the building; and once you came out, you never went back in. So, unless you'd stolen it when everybody was there watching, it couldn't have been you. Besides, I trusted Sherlock's instinct to trust you."

Looking very pleased with himself and Amy, Sherlock wagged his tail so hard it thumped against the chairs on either side of the aisle.

"Thank you," Amy said. There was too much to thank Dr. Schieber for to say anything else.

By then Mrs. Gorman had pulled out a family snapshot taken at the beach: Mr. and Mrs. Gorman, Sean, and a big Irish setter.

"Wow!" Sherlock said, wagging his tail even faster. "Look at those long legs!"

Dr. Schieber looked startled, then amused, then she shook Amy's hand. "Best of luck to all of you," she said. Then to Amy and Sherlock, she added, "Try to stay out of trouble."

"Yes," said Amy.

"Certainly," said Sherlock.

But even as he said it, his wagging tail swiped across the blackboard's chalk tray, knocking down an eraser.

Sean and Minneh both dove to get it and clunked their heads together. The eraser fell between their outstretched hands and hit the floor with a cloud of chalk dust. Mrs. Gorman leaned forward to make sure Sean was all right, and knocked over her opened purse, scattering its contents in the chalk dust. Mr. Gorman stood to help his wife, but the fifth-grade-sized chair clung to his considerably more than fifth-grade-sized bottom. The chair's legs caught in the legs of Amy's mom's desk, toppling it over, dumping out the books and papers and pens from inside, as well as Mom's purse from off the top, which clunked down on Mrs. Gorman's head.

Dr. Schieber had her I'm-getting-a-headache look as Sherlock repeated, "Certainly," and Amy once again said, "Yes."

Amy didn't think any of them really believed it for a minute.